THE QUANTITY

OF DESIRE

A novel by Payson R. Harris

LUNA EMUGIO

EX STULTITIA, SAPIENTIAM FIT

Cover art by Civetstranj
Cover and layout design by Nico Janssen

First published in 2021

ISBN: 978-1-7773642-1-2

TABLE OF CONTENTS

I

II

III

IV

V

I

LANDING

"It's the same sun," my mother whispered. Her wet breath brushed my ear, yet I strained to hear her quiet reassurance over the shouts of sailors and the cracks of shipping crates. "Whenever you miss home, look up and revel in its radiance. Its heat and light will caress you, and you'll remember our gods protect us here, too."

I don't remember our gods. I don't know if I ever did. She probably said it for herself as much as she said it for me. We both needed the consolation. That night, we sat in a cell so dark, I could only feel her hand against my face as she stroked me gently. Her hard fingertips slid through my fur to touch the skin beneath while her manacles clanked against my collar.

The next day, slavers separated us. A minotaur only sells as a curiosity, so why would anyone want two?

Then, I remember humans. Lots and lots of humans. Humans barking orders. Humans pulling leashes. Humans cracking whips.

Then darkness.

I walked through an arch of light into a giant ring, rows of eyes staring down at me. All the humans look the same in my memory. Knowing Castulo, there would have been different skin tones and genders throughout the audience, but now their features have blurred into a vague, genderless olive.

Except my future owner. I would not forget him.

Pale, tall, clean-shaven, entering middle-age. He sat neither slouched nor upright. He took no more than a glance at me as I dumbly followed the olive blob into the ring, the crack of whips still fresh in my mind. Instead, he studied everyone else as they whispered about my horns, my fur, and my hooves. That intrigued him.

A brightly dressed blob shouted that I was captured on the other side of the ocean, and that I, beast-like, would grow large and mighty. But I was yet a child and could be tamed and made to heel. Intelligent enough to follow orders, but dumb enough to keep my bonds once grown.

Perfect for anyone with a firm hand and a taste for the exotic.

The bidding was slow to start. The olive blobs whispered to those beside them, still not quite sure what to make of me. The other marvels from across the ocean—rare spices, novel magics, and intricate contraptions—were much easier to quantify.

What was a creature like me worth? I was strong, perhaps, but had no magical abilities. I was still too much a child for gladiatorial combat or sex work. Practically, it made no sense to purchase me; you could buy a dozen strong slaves for my starting price alone.

But having something others could desire but never possess? That is worth money.

And so, one by one, olive blobs opened their black mouths and shouted bids into the ring. Each shout spurred another blob into action, and soon one bid followed another in quick succession.

This made my owner's eyes sparkle.

Every other bidder looked at me with a hunger in their eyes that I could not bear. But my owner didn't so much as glance at me when he bid. Instead, he watched everyone else. When outbid, did they save their money for future auctions? Or did they work the numbers to bid again?

My owner watched more and more olive blobs check their books and bid again or shake their heads with a derision they tried so hard to believe. The Minotaur was desired. The minotaur—I—needed to be his.

Much later, during one of his speeches through which I was to look at him with wonder and remain completely silent, he explained my value: *What are a person's needs? A handful of roots, a tent, and a blanket. Even hermits have that. Civilization,* he said with a grand sweep of his arm, *is built on desire.*

Without desire, the back-breaking mining and the face-scorching smithing dissipate as the sword sits in a storehouse, unused. And how do we measure desire? He paused for a dramatic flourish. *By seeing what someone will pay for it!*

And people would pay for me.

But my owner would not pay a penny more than he needed to. He outbid anyone before they could even finish speaking, and they gave up quickly. They all knew he wanted me; they all knew he had the wealth to get me. As a result, he told me later, I was cheaper than if he hadn't bid at all.

Reputation, he said, is everything.

The gavel pounded as the brightly clothed olive blob shouted, "Sold!" And there I was: young, terrified, alone . . . and desired. And now, owned.

A sharp tug at my leash, and I was led back into the dark. I could hear the slow, heavy footsteps of the olive blob with the whip behind me. I counted the steps in the dark and wondered how close the whip was to my still-tender back. But I resisted the urge to turn around—I had learned that the hard way.

Finally, the dark passed into dim torchlight, and I was face-to-face with the slave master. He was a slave himself, branded and collared. He looked at me with a nonchalance touched lightly by compassion, as though he were passing yet another unfortunate beggar on the street.

"Your owner will pick you up after the auction is over," he said, "so you should make yourself ready for your new life." His voice was calm, and almost—but not quite—bored. "You can either make yourself miserable pining for some miracle of freedom that will never come, or you can accept your fate and take what happiness there is in this life. There are rewards from obedience, but none from the whip."

He waved me over to a corner of the room and prepared to greet the next slave. But I stood there, frozen.

In the day I had been in this land, I had been beaten and expected it. I had been broken and accepted it. But the sincerity of his short speech terrified me anew. There was no ruthless cruelty to make me obey, no terrifying posturing, just an apathetic bureaucrat giving a smidgeon of advice in the faint hope it will be of use.

My life unrolled before me. Today I would embrace obedience or embrace the whip. I had no knowledge of my owner, duties, or life, and I had no choice in any of them. I would accept them or be made to accept them.

It wasn't until years later that I realised his speech was a performance, as calculated and ruthless as the whips that lashed me. Other slaves were given the exact same speech, with the same drop of kindness in an ocean of indifference. Slaves who are broken bring back buyers.

Sincerity is another asset to be quantified and used.

"Him," an olive blob said, pointing at me. "Bring the minotaur to me."

I don't know how long had passed before the olive blob came. Olive blobs had come and gone and come again, callinvg names and carting slaves.

I scrambled to my feet as an olive blob walked over to me and unlocked my chain from the wall. Holding my chain like a leash, it led me through the darkness once again, past screams and the reek of unwashed flesh. Finally, we exited the market, and the sun burnt my eyes.

"Here he is, Mr. Galat," the blob said.

My eyes adjusted to the light, and there he was in front of me, his hand firm on my leash: my owner. He did not command the street as he had the ring, but he still radiated confidence.

He was flanked by two bodyguards, a man and a woman. Both towered over me in scarred armor inlaid with gold. Even in the guarded lot of the auction house, they scouted the route with attentive eyes.

We approached a glossy black carriage, its wrought iron frame gracefully curved around the thick wood of its cabin. A few gems, larger than any I had seen before, were inset in its corners, glittering in the sunlight.

My owner glanced at his bodyguards. They nodded, then climbed up the front of the carriage, leaving me alone with him.

He turned to me and looked down, impossibly tall. He studied me with cold eyes, and I bit my lip. I tried to remember my mother's voice and her words of reassurance. It's the same sun, I told myself.

"I suspect you're smarter than they gave you credit for," he murmured. "That's good." Then he crouched down and looked into my eyes. Neither cruel nor kind, his eyes took in everything they saw and cataloged it away for future analysis.

I stared back into his eyes, too afraid to look away. I wanted to cry but had learned it would only make things worse.

When he spoke, his voice was firm and steady, beyond question or doubt. "My name is Jon Galat," he said. "You're mine now, but you need not fear me. I will be fair to you. I will not work you to illness or death, I will not subject you to any unnecessary cruelty, and I will not ask you to do anything I have not done myself to reach my station.

"I will show you off to visiting dignitaries, and you will treat them with respect. I will require you to fetch books and refreshments for me, and I like an audience as I talk." He broke eye contact, staring into the high walls of Castulo. "For now, that will be the extent of your duties. When I do not have need of you, you will have the run of my estate. It is large and beautiful, and I hope you will enjoy it." He looked back into my eyes to ensure I understood.

I swallowed and willed my head to nod, but it would not obey me.

He put his hand on my shoulder. It was not heavy, but neither was it light. "Slave though you are, I do not believe in forcing people into a life ill-suited to them. If you do not consent, I will sell you back to the auction house, and I will hope that your next buyer will have work more suitable to you."

I tried to swallow a sob but failed. I cried hard, my breath catching in the back of my throat. He pulled a handkerchief from his pocket and brushed away my tears in quick, efficient wipes.

I know now this was meant to be consoling.

When I stopped crying, he continued. "I understand this has been difficult for you. I will give you time to adapt to your new life. But I need an answer from you now." His gaze did not break from mine. "Will you abide by the terms of our agreement?"

This was the choice the slave-master had spoken of. *There are rewards from obedience, but none from the whip.* I would live in a strange land, obeying a strange man.

Or I would go back into the screaming darkness.

It took me a few tries to squeak out a single, "Yes."

"Good," he declared. Then he tapped my manacles and said, "Phuta-ti." My manacles and collar opened and fell off, clanking in the dust at my feet. "Trust is an essential part of any transaction," he said, "and I will start by trusting you. Keep my trust, and life will be pleasant for both of us."

He climbed into the carriage, then turned and offered me a hand up. I looked at it and imagined running away, biting his hand, or just sitting and crying for my mother.

"Come now," he said. "Let us go to your new home. I purchased some toys and books for you to use on your journey." He paused. "Can you read?"

I nodded.

"Good. That will be beneficial to your work." He smiled. It was too smooth to be natural. "Now, grab my hand." His tone was gentle, but I had learned to recognise a command.

I complied.

He had not lied, I saw. Brightly painted wizards and warriors, balls on string, scopperls, and rolling hoops lay atop books of fables, astronomy, finance, and etiquette.

"I know this has been difficult for you, so I will leave you to play as you wish." Then he turned to his book and forgot about me.

Or so I thought at the time. Now, I know he thought he was being kind, perhaps even generous. He thought I was overwhelmed from the torture of the slave pens and the chaos of the auction. Thus, he allowed me to settle myself away from the demands of others.

He wasn't completely wrong. I had been made to obey anyone who grabbed my leash. I had been bought by a strange man and thrust into a life I knew nothing about. I had been broken by whips and sneers and had my future stripped from me.

This was my first moment to be myself, to breathe, and I could barely open my lungs to do so. I suppose I was overwhelmed, as Jon presumed.

But what I really was, was alone.

LIFE

"I do not condone him calling you a monster," Jon said, his voice quiet but unyielding. "He was cruel." He crouched down and stared into my eyes. "I am sorry you must endure this, but endure this you must. You have a job to do. And you will carry it out."

Over the months I had lived with Jon, he had made sure I knew how to do my job—and that I would carry it out. So, I sniffled, rubbed my muzzle, and tried to suppress my tears. But I could still hear the dignitary's voice, wondering how Jon could bear to live in the same house as a monster. Only the polished stone and carved oak door of this hallway separated us as he waited in Jon's study.

"Here," Jon said, and handed me a handkerchief.

As I blew my nose, I wondered if Jon had ever been a child. I could not imagine him any way but as he was.

"Now I must go back and discuss business with this man. I trust you to know what to do."

I nodded. This man had been cruel, but I bore indignities from even the most innocent of visitors. I endured their curious pokes and prods, touching my fur and grabbing my horns. I stood impassively while they asked Jon questions about me as though I were a statue. And, when asked, I said whatever they wished to hear in perfect formal speech.

"Good," Jon said. He turned and walked into his study.

I wiped the snot from my muzzle and took another breath to steady myself. As Jon had taught me, I told myself that I just had to fetch wine and food and I would be free. I could not master my emotions as he did, but the thought did calm me.

I went down to the kitchen and asked the chef what was being prepared.

"Deer," he told me.

I nodded and remembered what Jon had told me about deer. *It's like beef, but finer and leaner,* he had said. *An elegant red pairs nicely.*

I climbed down to the cellar, grateful my fur kept me warm. I looked through the reds, past Tecks, Oseras, and Aomes before settling on an Usulo. I took it and grabbed two glasses to go with it. On the way back up, I grabbed a plate of delicate pastries, steam still rising off them.

When I arrived at Jon's door, I put down the plate, and knocked.

"Come in, Chase," Jon said.

I opened the door, picked up the plate, and walked into the study. Jon sat behind his desk, facing the door, and the man sat across from him. A few books lay open on the table; judging from the empty spaces on the Grenadil bookshelf, this meeting had something to do with mining.

I put down the plate on the ornate ebony desk, then poured two glasses of wine. I handed one to Jon, and then, with a steadying breath, handed the other to the man across from him.

He glared at me through bushy brows before slowly reaching out. Then he snatched it. His hand darted back with the wine, and some spilled onto the desk. I grabbed a cloth from my waistband and wiped it up before it stained.

"Thank you, Chase," Jon said. "That will be all."

I forced myself to walk slowly out of the room, then gently closed the door behind me.

Then I ran.

I ran all the way back to my room. I leapt into bed and buried my face in my pillow. I remembered the time that, over the screams of defiance and the sobs of obedience, over the cracks of whips and canes, and over the laugh of men who revelled in my tears, I could hear the clank of my mother's manacles against my collar, I could feel the wetness of her breath against my ear, and I didn't have a hole in my heart.

I suppose I could've been treated worse. Many others were—and still are.

Jon Galat was emotionally obtuse, but he hired the best priests and doctors when I was sick, instructed the chef to cook food I enjoyed, and provided time to play and rest.

He was the closest thing to a parent I had.

I knew that, by buying me, he financed the slavers who ripped me from my mother. But, in my lonely, child's mind, I also knew he freed me from the horror of the pens and whips and tried to treat me well. He cared for me—in his strange, self-absorbed way.

And, at his manor, I found what I truly needed: a friend.

"What are you?" the boy asked the first time I met him.

I stood silently, enduring his stare as I did those of the dignitaries. I was used to their manner of questioning. But his next words surprised me.

"You have horns! That's so amazing! Could you stab someone with them?" He skipped around me, examining me from every angle. His feet barely touched the grass. "Do you speak?"

I nodded.

"My name's Bri," he said, holding out his hand.

I took it. "Chase," I said. He looked at me as though he wanted more, so I finally added, "I'm a minotaur."

"That's amazing!" Bri shouted. "My mom and dad are Jon's bodyguards. They're amazing," he said, gazing through the forest that surrounded Jon's manor. "They were real heroes in their time and have medals from hundreds of villages they saved from orcs and goblins and trolls."

He puffed out his chest. "I'm gonna be an archer like my father. He can drive an arrow straight through a breastplate at a hundred paces!

"But no one can beat my mom with a sword and shield. Once, she was ambushed by twenty orcs while her party slept. And then do you know what she did?" He looked into my eyes, giggling. "She said she was sorry the orcs' dying screams had woken up the rest of the party."

I couldn't help but smile as he laughed.

"Wanna be my sidekick, Chase? I need someone to watch my back while I save people with my arrows."

I nodded.

He grabbed my hand. "Then come on!"

He pulled me along a little path through the forest and into a clearing. He picked up a toy bow with cork-tipped arrows from a pile of wooden weapons and turned to me. "There are a whole bunch of monsters coming at us," he said. "You protect me from them until I can kill their general with my arrows. He's a demon-god from deep in hell, with horns, fire, pitchfork, and, well"—Bri waved his arms as he tried to think of the things a demon-god would have—"everything!"

"I will protect you," I said. It reverberated through my core.

"Amazing," he said, then he smiled at me. It looked like the widest, most pure smile that would ever be.

I would do anything to see that smile.

"Let's get you a shield," Bri said. He picked up a wooden shield from a pile of weapons and gave it to me.

I took it and held it against my chest. "I will protect you," I said again.

Bri smiled, but not as wide as before. Had I said it wrong?

"If you're gonna hold it against your chest, you gotta grip the far handle," he said, pointing to the edge of the shield. "That way your elbow isn't so exposed."

I gripped the far handle and said it again: "I will protect you."

"Yes," he cried. "Amazing!"

My heart fluttered.

He went back to the pile of weapons and pulled out a wooden sword. "Now try this," he said, thrusting it into my hand.

My shoulder almost popped out of its socket as I swung the sword with a dramatic war squeak that would strike concern into the most timid of mice.

"No, no, no," he muttered. He put his hand on his chin and paced back and forth. "The sword looks all wrong on you." He scuffed the dirt with his foot. "You're a minotaur. You're big and hairy and horny and scary. But swords aren't scary."

What could I do if my body were wrong?

"I know what you need!" he shouted, already running across the clearing. He grabbed a wooden axe then bounded back across the grass to me.

He threw away the sword, then thrust the axe into my open hand. My fingers closed around the shaft, their keratinous tips digging into the wood.

"Amazing!" he shouted. Then he spoke so fast he tripped over his words. "A minotaur's got to have an axe. Sword's a weapon of grace, yeah, but look! With that massive axe any demon would be terrified to come near you! And those who do, you'll block with your shield while I destroy them with my arrows."

A minotaur's got to have an axe. I rested the axe on my shoulder, trying to look big and tough. "No one will get through me," I declared in the meanest voice I could.

I have never meant anything as much as I meant those words.

"Now, you stand there," he said, pointing to a spot about ten paces away, "and get ready." He laid out his cork-tipped arrows in front of him. "Here come the demons!"

He fired an arrow over my shoulder, and it landed in the grass at my feet. "That demon-god is tough! He swatted my arrow aside!"

Bri looked at me. "They're right on top of you Chase! Block them with your shield and I'll take them out!"

I lifted my shield and let out a squeak of war.

Bri shot another arrow, and it hit me in the back. "My arrow tears through their ranks!" he shouted.

I swung my axe a few times, earning cheers from Bri.

"The demon-god is right on top of you, Chase! He's beating you to the ground!"

I fell to the ground, holding my shield up to defend myself. An arrow sailed over my head.

"I got him! You distracted him while my arrow went right through his eye!" Bri ran around the clearing, his bow lifted in the air. He whooped at the top of his lungs, and the trees carried the sound back to us as a chorus.

I followed him around the clearing, as I would follow him wherever he led.

When I wasn't bowing before dignitaries or playing with Bri, my time was spent with Jon, in his study. He would talk, and I would listen.

"People assume that general intelligence and knowledge are enough to tackle any problem," he told me after one particularly frustrating conversation with a mine foreman. "But they aren't."

He sighed and sat down heavily. "You spend months working on your perfect plan, and something so small it has no name throws off all your calculations. The rock you dig through experiences the slightest shift—and your mine collapses on itself.

"Some learned fools look down at those they see as their inferiors, swinging their pickaxes in the dark every day. Sometimes, those learned fools are more intelligent, but intelligence means nothing if you have not felt your pickaxe shiver as it strikes the rock.

"Every system is a dense web of delicate feedback mechanisms. Every day, billions of decisions ripple out unto eternity. By buying an axe, I raise the demand for iron, smithing, logging, and woodworking. People who already consider those jobs see an opportunity and take it. This raises the demand for textiles, engineers, tanners . . .

"No matter how brilliant, no one can understand the whole web; no one can see how a smith in Castulo connects to a teacher in Narasi. But they do. That's the beauty of the web.

"Our world is shaped by every single person who lives in it."

And so, the days, months, and years dragged on. I performed my duties and learned of economics and business. I loved Bri with the ferocity that only a lonely child can have. When Bri was busy and Jon had no need of me, I would lie in the grass, look into the sky, and tell myself, "It's the same sun." I would imagine a life with Bri, setting off on adventures and protecting him until he could save the day. My life was not happy, but it had its pleasures, and I endured it.

In my childish naivety, I thought that it would go on that way forever.

DEATH

"And you say he's self-aware?" Though Valence spoke to Jon, his green eyes studied me from my hooves to my horns. I stared ahead blankly, as though his gaze didn't make my skin crawl.

"He is," Jon replied. He looked at me over Valence's shoulder, the enchanted light of the hallway flattening his features.

"How can you tell?"

"He can speak for himself."

"That is hard to believe," Valence said. "Though I have heard of orcs speaking broken English. I suppose even beasts are capable of some intelligence."

"Chase is more intelligent than most people I know." Jon's voice betrayed no emotion.

"Really? A furry creature like this?"

"Please allow me the indulgence of a demonstration," Jon said. "Chase, if you please?"

"The price of anything is determined by its demand and supply," I intoned with just enough feeling to show this was not mere memorization. "Thus, price has two functions: it signals the availability or lack thereof of any product and allocates scarce resources to their most productive and valuable uses."

The magistrate stepped back, his heavy footstep echoing off the stone walls despite the carpet. He opened his mouth, then closed it. When he finally spoke, his voice was calm and controlled, as though he had never been surprised. "Does he understand what he's saying?"

"He does," Jon said idly. "I can ask him to explain it for you, if you need it."

"No, I do not." Anger and embarrassment flashed across his face. But Jon had a plan.

"I thought not," Jon replied. "I know a fellow brilliant mind when I meet one. But few people are as astute as we are, so one gets used to making . . . allowances."

"We are a rare breed," Valence said. He practically preened himself.

John smiled at me. His prized bull had worked as intended. I could not resist a swell of pride.

"That's why I can't wait to hear your thoughts on my proposed factory. Those fools on your council have ridiculous fears, but I know I can count on you for an intelligent analysis," Jon said.

"You have no idea of the injudicious stupefaction I endure." Valence sighed, drawing it out for longer than I thought possible. "But yes, I have investigated your proposal thoroughly, and deduced many forms through which we can ensure this is mutually beneficial." He turned away from me to look back at Jon.

Jon put on his practiced smile. "Excellent. Let us retire to my study, where we can discuss this in comfort." He put his hand on the magistrate's back and lead him down the hall. Then, Jon casually called over his shoulder, "Chase, a bottle of my rarest wine."

Jon continued talking to the magistrate as they walked. "This wine is a true exotic treat. Imported from an island far south, where the locals ride waves as we ride horses. A wine as rare as our intelligence."

Jon laid it on thick, but it was working. Valence took every compliment and beamed.

The wine was rare, but not quite in the way Jon implied. Few people wanted wine from some unknown island. Jon had simply tried it while travelling and developed a liking for it. He did not generally approve of lying, but for Valence he would make an exception, and Jon had to get Valence on his side.

Rent seeking, Jon had said with more venom than he had for murder. *Valence is an odious, narcissist of a man. He's supposed to ensure the quality of magical enterprises in his home of Witjour Tops, but of course he finds only the magic guild meets the safety requirements. And for his judicious oversight, he receives custom enchantments and is a guest of honour at all guild events.*

But a coven of old witches wants to move there. The hot springs soothe their aches and pains, and we have no better magic against the ravages of age. But the guild will brook no competition against their business, and Valence carries out their will.

How can I compete with such grift? Jon grinned. *I serve a market no one considered before. The guild's enchantments are bespoke, opulent jewels of wealth and status. By selling to the common peasant, we harm not their business. And, with each witch casting an easily memorised part of a larger spell, they can create simple, cheap, and effective enchantments, such as self-cleaning dishes and clothes, that make life better—and me lots of money.*

I ran down the hall, knowing my job was almost done. Fetch the wine, and I would be free to play with Bri and Rorvin, Valence's son. Bri was always happy to have the children of guests join our adventures and help us save the world.

I climbed down the stairs to the cellar thinking of my last adventure with Bri, when I had jumped in front of a ballista spear in order to save him. The spear stuck deep in my chest and blasted me through the air to die at Bri's feet as he fired his arrow right into the Ogre-chieftain's belly, killing it.

The wine retrieved, I climbed back upstairs, and entered Jon's study.

Valence turned to look at me as I carried the bottle in my fingertips. He still marvelled at my existence. I could feel, rather than see, Jon's smirk.

I poured two glasses, then re-corked the wine and placed it on the sideboard. As I left the room, I bowed deeply, and heard Jon propose a toast. "To reasonable men!" he shouted. But I didn't linger to hear more.

I had Bri to find.

I scampered down the stairs, ran through the yard, and followed the path into the forest. As I approached the clearing where Bri and I played, I heard an unfamiliar voice that must be Rorvin. I ran toward the sound, but as I drew closer, I realised it was not the joyous shouts of play.

"—at pretend, like an infant? My father had me using a real sword when I was five."

I ran faster.

"Fighting demons like in some fantasy book? Only a child could enjoy such puerile stories."

Through leaves, I saw the blue of Rorvin's tunic and the brown hair on the back of his head. I sprinted into the clearing; Rorvin held a wooden sword, cocked. He swung down, and it thudded against Bri's head. Bri groaned.

"Stop it!" I screamed. My hands balled. I lowered my head and glared at him through my eyebrows. "Leave Bri alone!"

Rorvin turned toward me. A few years older than Bri and I, he towered over Bri's fallen form. His smile was broad and cruel. "Is this your friend, Brimark? The one who uses the axe? The little slave cow who follows you around?" He laughed, long and loud. It carried through the trees, echoing softly. "You really are pathetic."

He swung the sword again, harder this time. It hit Bri with a wrenching thunk, and Bri sprawled onto the ground, blood gushing from his temple and flowing down his face.

Rorvin was going to kill Bri, I thought, and then I'd be all alone. My eyes locked on the blue of Rorvin's tunic. My muzzle snarled. His tunic grew larger as my hooves pounded the ground, drowning out everything but the rushing blood in my ears. The dirt beneath me disappeared as Rorvin turned toward me.

"Really?" He laughed, and the wooden sword smashed into my shoulder. My hooves slid along the ground as I fought to stay upright. "Wha—?"

The ground shred the side of my face and dirt filled my mouth. I saw nothing but the green of grass and heard nothing but my ragged breath.

Something jerked my head around by my horns, and then I heard a retch and the splatter of blood.

I lay there, panting, until I finally heard Bri say, "By Balantor's blade."

Bri was alive. The tension drained out of my body, and my breathing slowed. I tried to get up but was held down by my horns, and I heard Rorvin scream.

"Chase, don't move," Brimark said. "Krek," he cursed, "this is bad." Bri grabbed my head and pulled me back. Rorvin screamed again, and blood poured onto the grass in front of my eyes.

Finally, I came free.

"Rorvin, I'm going to try to stop the bleeding." Bri's words were clipped, his voice squeaking.

I got up and saw Bri's red hands on Rorvin's belly. Blood seeped between his fingers, covering his wrists. His hands moved furtively over the wound, spreading the blood around in a futile attempt to stop the bleeding. Rorvin screamed again.

I inspected the wound on Bri's head. It was nothing more than a little cut. A trail of blood dripped down from it, falling off his face, splattering against his hands, and sinking into the gaping hole in the middle of Rorvin's chest.

"Chase, take off your shirt," Bri said. I complied, then held the shirt in my hand, awaiting further instruction like a golem.

"Put it on the wound!" His voice squeaked. He pulled his hands away so I could place my shirt over the hole. Bri pushed it into the blood. It was red in seconds.

Rorvin gurgled.

"It's not working. It's not working. Krek, Krek, Krek, Krek, Krek!" Bri pushed harder into Rorvin's belly, and Rorvin coughed up blood. "Get my parents!" Bri screamed. "Run!"

I leapt over root and bush, ducked under branch and vine, and charged through web and leaf. My chest burned, but I kept running.

I banged on the door of Bri's cottage, growling insensibly. The door opened and Bri's mother, Avinna, stood there, her light hair loose around her broad shoulders.

"Chase," she said, then saw the webs on my face and the blood on my horns. "What happened. Is Brimark all right?"

The words came out of my mouth at once. "Rorvin was swinging a sword at him and then I was running and then the dirt was in my face and then Bri's hands were red and there was blood dripping on his shirt from his head and he told me to get you and I ran here."

Her face went white. "Lead the way," she said tersely. "Run!"

I ran, my steps short and quick. She followed with long and powerful strides. As we approached the clearing, Rorvin screamed, and I was left looking at her hair bouncing behind her.

"Brimark—I was so worried," I heard her say through the trees. When I caught up, she was holding him tightly, her lips pressed to his forehead, bloody handprints all over her.

"Mom, it's Rorvin," Bri said. Then he cried.

Avinna pulled a needle from her belt and attached a string to it. "He's lost a lot of blood. Get me an apophlegmatism. Sage or tobacco. You'll find them in the kitchen." Now that Brimark was safe, her voice was controlled and even. "Go, Brimark."

Bri turned slowly, then ran.

She took my shirt off Rorvin and placed it on the grass beside him. "Kneel here." Avinna pointed beside her.

I kneeled. Rorvin was getting quieter. He mumbled and moaned.

"Grab his belly in your hands and pinch it together."

I reached into the blood and tried to pinch the wound together, but my fingers slipped off the slick skin.

Avinna pushed my hands out of the way and plunged her own into the blood. She pulled the skin together in her fingers, then said, "Hold this, and don't move."

I took hold of the skin and watched the red travel up my brown fur.

Avinna looked at her hands. They shook, but she took a breath and they stilled. Then, needle in hand, she reached in.

The needle moved quickly but precisely; it never went further than needed to complete the stitch. She pulled on the thread, and the wound began to close. She moved my hands and completed the suture. The flow of blood slowed. Avinna took off her shirt and pressed it against the wound.

But Rorvin was pale and still.

She grabbed my hands and forced them against her shirt and Rorvin's belly. "Press hard," she said.

I complied. I couldn't feel any warmth through the shirt.

"Brimark should be back any second now," she said to herself. She looked back to the cottage, trying to peer through the trees that blocked the view.

A few moments later, Bri came running into the clearing, his breathing fast and shallow. He handed a bundle of thin, pointy leaves to her. "Sage," he panted, "from the kitchen."

"Good," she said. "Now breathe." Then she leaned over Rorvin's mouth, opened it, put some of the leaves in, and massaged his neck. He murmured but didn't chew or swallow.

She took the leaves from Rorvin's mouth, put them in her own, and chewed them. Then she spat it into his mouth and massaged his neck. He swallowed.

She did that a few more times. Each time it became harder and harder to make him swallow.

Finally, the leaves were gone, and Rorvin was still becoming paler.

Avinna looked down at Rorvin and frowned. She wiped her forehead with the back of her hand, leaving a trail of blood.

"I don't know what else to do," she said.

HEARTBREAK

"I will kill him!" Valence's face was dark, and his fists were clenched. He strode across the clearing to me, his narrow eyes as sharp as a blade. "Give me a sword!" he thundered. He looked around the forest but saw only Bri's wooden weapons.

I clutched my knees to my chest as I lay in the grass.

"He is my slave, and I will deal with him as I see fit," Jon declared.

"He murdered my son!" Valence grabbed a wooden sword and swung it at me. I put up my arms and the wood hit my forearm, hard. The pain shot down into my hand and up into my shoulder. I cried.

"Avinna, disarm him," Jon said, and she leapt between us, grabbed the wooden sword by the blade, and twisted. It popped out of Valence's hands.

Valence turned his fury on Jon. "How dare you stop me from killing this disgusting beast!"

"Is this how you deal with crime?" Jon asked, his voice unyielding. "Do you allow retribution without trial?"

"He is a slave! A feral beast!"

"He is my slave. Not yours," Jon said. Then, a touch quieter, "Not until the law says otherwise."

"You think the law will protect a slave?" Valence stomped over to Jon, his nose almost pressing against Jon's own. Droplets of spittle covered Jon as Valence screamed, "Are you that thick?"

Jon gazed back into Valence's eyes as though he were talking about the finer points of iron smelting—but his chest rose and fell with deliberate movement. "I do not think it will. He will likely be executed. But not until a judge rules that it be so."

Valence started to say, "Then let me execute—"

But Jon knew how to command attention. "A society without rule of law is a society without the ability to trust." Jon's clear voice rang through the woods. "And a society without trust falls to barbarism. No, we will go before a judge and determine the legal course of action."

Valence growled. "May Yryja grind your skin off with salt, bathe you in scorpion peppers, and feed you to her rats."

With narrow eyes and a creased brow, Valence stared into Jon as though he could will Yryja to fulfill his curse now. Then he stormed off into the trees.

"You will wish you had let me kill him!" Valence shouted, then he was gone.

Jon took a few loud, shuddering breaths, his head arcing back as he exhaled.

My arm ached from Valence's blow, and the pain radiated into my chest. But I buried my muzzle in the grass, willing it to muffle my tears. I prayed I would disappear, and no one would ever find me. I could just watch over Bri, and never let anyone harm him again.

"So, Chase," Jon said, his voice devoid of emotion. "Why did you kill him?"

I swallowed my tears and squeezed my eyes shut, praying once more to be whisked away. But the deep and rich scent of the earth never left my nose. Finally, I rolled onto my back and looked into the sky. "He hit Bri with the sword," I said. "There was so much blood. Rorvin kept saying, 'You're pathetic.' I was so scared he was going to kill Bri," I said. "And . . . I just charged."

"I see." Jon paused. "Avinna? Do you know anything more?"

"Sadly, no. When I arrived, everything was already over. I tried to save him, but with such a massive puncture wound in the belly, there was not much I could do."

"I see," Jon said. I don't think I had ever heard him repeat himself like that.

"My negotiations are over now." His voice was quiet, but firm. "Avinna, any ideas?"

She looked at the grass. "No," she said, "I'm sorry. This is beyond me. Point me at something to stab and I'm your girl. Politics? You'll want my husband, Marcus, for that."

Jon nodded. "I see." He breathed again. "Take Bri and fetch Marcus, then." He thought for a second more. "Then take care of your son. Any child . . ." Jon stared at me.

"I can take Chase too," Avinna said.

"Thank you, Avinna," Jon said, his voice low. "Tell Marcus I will be in my study."

Avinna watched Jon walk off before she took Bri's hand in hers. Then she turned to me. Her eyes examined my bloody horns, bloody hands, and bloody fur.

She paused, her lips pursed. I think that, for the first time, she realised I had killed a boy. I hadn't meant to kill him, she must have known. I had tried to protect her son, she knew for certain. Rorvin had cruelly bullied him, she had ample evidence.

But he was just a boy.

Then she closed her eyes. "Come, Chase," she said.

I took her calloused yet soft hand in my keratinous fingers and walked with her.

The forest passed, a splotchy mass of green and brown.

"Don't worry," she said, looking straight ahead. Her hand gripped mine. "I've met many mages who could turn the world to their will and slice through the fabric of reality with their mind. But none have honed their mind as sharp as Jon's."

I knew how smart Jon was, but he had spoken of my death as though it had already been decided. I had liked to pretend I was just another employee of his. He treated me as one, so the lie had held. But even Jon was beholden to the law, and, in its eyes, I wasn't a person.

I had tried so hard to take the *rewards from obedience*. I had imagined some joy, some safety from being as good as I could be. Instead, I would never live to be an adult.

I tried to breathe, like Jon had taught me, and let the emotion pass. I tried to distract myself by thinking of playing with Bri. Instead, I cried.

When we reached her cabin, Avinna took a long, serious look at it, then led us inside. There were a few small windows that let in enough light to see the main room, with a table and chairs for the family and a small firepit for cooking and warmth.

Avinna breathed as though she were preparing for battle. Her eyes followed the blood down our bodies. "Chase, Brimark, take off your clothes," she said. "I'll warm some water for the bath."

We complied.

She walked to the firepit, added a few logs, and uncovered the embers buried beneath the ash. The logs ignited, and she took a pot of water and placed it above the fire. She grabbed two more pots and walked to the door. "I'll be back shortly," she said, then left.

While she was gone, I tried to think of a way out of this. But all I could imagine was myself on the gallows while onlookers talked of a monster who could only rage and murder.

Avinna walked back in, the pots filled with water. She replaced the pot above the fire with one from the river, and then poured the water into the bath. She glanced at us, picked up the two empty pots, and walked out again.

I looked at Bri, willing words to come. But an oppressive weight stilled my chest. I could barely breathe. I wanted to tell Bri everything would be all right. That, for as long as he lived, I would be by his side; I would follow him around from town to town as he vanquished demons and monsters, and as the town adulated him, he'd look down at me, and smile.

"I thought he was going to kill you," I finally managed to say.

I doubted the words as soon as they were out of my muzzle. I hadn't really thought at all. I had seen him in danger, then panicked.

Bri's eyes met mine, then he turned and looked at the floor, his hands, and the pile of our clothes. "I felt so helpless," he said. "I was pathetic."

His words squeezed my heart. "It's my fault. I was supposed to be your shield. You could have downed him at a hundred paces with your bow. He caught you by surprise, that's all." Whatever would make him smile, I would say it.

He held me then, his head against my shoulder. "If you die," Bri said, "it's because I couldn't defend myself."

"Boys," Avinna warned as she walked into the room with more water.

"Mom," Bri cried, "would they really kill Chase? I know he's a slave, but—"

"Come, both of you," Avinna interrupted. "Let's get you cleaned up."

She poured the two pots she was carrying into the tub, and then took the water off the fire and poured it in too, filling the tub.

Bri had seen my naked body many times as we splashed about in the river, but today he studied my blood-matted fur. My blood-soaked horns.

"Jon will figure something out," Avinna said. "He always does."

"Mom—" Bri began, but Avinna seized us and led us to the tub.

"Now get in," she said.

We climbed into the tub in silence, then sat looking at each other, our bodies stiff.

"Let's get the blood off you," Avinna said. She walked over to the side of the room and returned with two sponges, handing one to each of us.

I watched the blood sluice off Bri's skin while I scrubbed at the blood stuck in my fur as though it were a scar. As we washed, the water gradually grew darker. I had imagined it would turn red with the blood. But as the last of the blood finally scrubbed off my fur, the water turned black.

TRUST

The edge of the stone stair dug coldly into my belly as Bri and I listened to the voices seeping through the large crack beneath the door of Jon's study. Bri held me close, his arm around my back, and helped me stay still. I breathed soft and shallow, straining to hear every word.

"We can appease them," said Avinna's powerful voice. "Chase used his horns, and a slave can't have a weapon. We can cut them off and show the judge he's no threat."

"Would Valence be appeased by anything but death?" said Jon's measured voice. "Until Valence is appeased, the law will not be either. Chase is a slave, and even I did not fully appreciate what that meant until now."

"Chase acted as a slave should, protecting a citizen," said Marcus's clear, melodic voice. "A youthful overreaction? Perhaps. But of love, not malice. If the judge understands that, they will see he is no threat to society."

"Will the judge see a boy striving to protect the people he loves?" Jon asked. "Or will they see a raging monster?"

"They do not know him as we do," Marcus said. "I will vouch for him."

"I, too, have seen him hold his temper through humiliation and insult," Jon said. "And yet, this time, he acted with rage and fear. How can we argue that he won't do what he very clearly did?"

Bri's hand dug into my side. His body was warm against mine. Still,

I was cold.

"A single incident," Marcus said.

"Have you met a minotaur before, Marcus?" Jon's voice sounded calm, but his words were overenunciated. "Do you know what they are like in adulthood? Perhaps this is just a hint of what is to come."

I held my breath.

"I have always assumed that his mind is like ours," Jon said. "But now I must ask myself, will his rage grow uncontrollable?"

The edge of the stair forced the air from my lungs.

"Do you really believe that?" Marcus asked.

"No," Jon said so quietly I could barely hear. "But I can't argue against it, either."

I pressed my muzzle into the stone. My nose felt like it was freezing to the rock.

"Then what do we do?" Avinna asked.

Jon hesitated. "I do not know. I am lost in my own mind, building structures of logic I cannot believe." I heard something fleshy hit wood.

"I have always taken my little corner of the world and counted and catalogued every blade of manicured grass. Other people could deal with the rest. And I found so much success that I almost forgot there was a whole other world I had ignored.

"And now I discover that I studied my little corner from an untended garden, whose vines have grown around me and pinned me to the ground."

There was a long silence, then. Bri took my hand and pulled me away; we had to be in bed by the time the meeting was over.

I remember little of the next few days. I ambled around in a daze, by turns anxious and numb.

Bri tried to help, creating fantastical battles in which I could protect him. Yet I could not keep them in my mind. Whether ogres, demons, goblins, or the gods themselves, the enemies we fought would blend together, and I'd swing my axe low to hit a goblin when I should have swung high for an ogre.

In the end, I would lie in the grass with Bri holding my hand. I'd look up at the sky and whisper, "It's the same sun." And then, at night,

I'd go back to my room, cry, and try to sleep.

"You say you were scared for Brimark," the constable told me, lean and dressed in grey. "Sure, I can see that as part of it—after all, he's your friend." He crossed his arms. "But don't you run from things you're afraid of?"

I remembered one of Jon's speeches, and repeated it. "Feeling is the impetus of action, true, but reason decides the appropriate response. I . . ." My voice failed me as I had to speak for myself.

This constable had come to gather facts for the case, or so Jon had said. But there had been a look in his eye as he introduced us.

I understood that look now.

He leaned forward, staring into my eyes with big black pupils. "And your reason told you to kill Rorvin?"

"No," I whispered. My shoulders pulled into my body, and my head sank into my chest.

"So, if it wasn't reasonable, it was emotional. And you say you were scared."

"Yes." I could barely hear my own voice.

"So, if you saw a dragon, you'd charge it because you were scared? You would, terrified, run into its fiery breath and down its gaping maw?"

I tried to think of something to say, but my mind was blank.

"Fear begets avoidance." He glared right through me. "You charged. That's anger. Rage. Wouldn't you agree?"

"No, I—"

"If you were scared, why didn't you run away?"

"I—"

"You thought no one should hurt your friend and live."

I cried.

"How old are you?"

I tried to answer around my sobs. "I—I'm—"

"It says here you're about thirteen. Thirteen!" His hand hit the table. I flinched.

"And already so big. As big as Rorvin was, and he was older. Your species must have a lot of rage, being so powerful. Maybe you feel we humans are weaker than you, and you've the right to deal with us as you will."

He listened to me cry.

"I thought so," he finally concluded, and marked it down on his sheet: *killed in anger.*

I had seen little of Jon over the days since Rorvin's death. He told me I was free from my duties, and I should do whatever I needed to take care of myself.

I did not know what that meant, so I simply did what I always did until one morning I awoke to a note under my door.

Come see me. I will be in my study. —Jon Galat

I dressed and climbed the stairs, my stomach tight. When I opened the door, he was writing in his notebook; he closed it quickly.

"Please, Chase, would you take a seat?" He spoke to me as one of his visitors, with grace and reverence.

I sat.

Jon stared at his notebook before he looked up, and his small, grey eyes met mine. "It does not look good," he began. "You thought you were protecting Brimark, and that might save you under normal circumstances. We could argue that you were a good slave, trying to defend the life of a compatriot of your owner."

Jon's eyes looked at me with compassion—just like he had practiced in the mirror. But his hands were clasped together so hard that the edges of his fingers were white.

"Slaves have the right to argue justifiable homicide when defending themselves or others, but no slave has escaped the gallows doing so," Jon said. "In cases where leniency is called for, the solution has been to keep them out of court. For example, if Rorvin had been a bandit, everyone involved would acknowledge you had done your duty, and there would be no record of you having killed anyone."

I nodded as much as my stiff neck would allow.

"But Valence has built connections for many years. He has people in power talking about how Rorvin was noble, generous, and would have become the greatest swordsman in Orachim."

Jon looked down at his notebook, his eyes following the coiled spine.

"Chase," he said, "I trusted you to make better decisions. Self-control is not the suppression of emotion, but the ability to prioritise our longer-term desires over our short-sighted impulses. It is that from which all other virtues flow." He looked into my eyes. "Do you understand?"

I swallowed. "Yes."

"Good," he said. Then he stood and turned away from me, stepping to the window at the back of the room.

I stared at his flat shoulders in silence.

"I," he began, then stopped.

He clasped his hands behind his back. Then clasped them in front of his body.

"I am not good at many things, Chase. In my own way, I am brilliant, and have never met my equal. And yet, everyone else understood things that always left me baffled. So, I told myself I could forget about them. Other people gave love and friendship to the world; I gave jobs and wealth.

"It was a good solution, I thought. Government passes laws that reflect the people's priorities. Therefore, good businesspeople concern themselves not with morality, but legality. So long as I operated within the law, I did good.

"I knew the system wasn't perfect. Market failures, I called them. Sometimes, a trade hurts those who were not part of it. Sometimes, we must make decisions without the information we need. Sometimes, government attempts to ameliorate a problem but makes it worse. And, sometimes, regulators who ensure honesty and compliance become corrupt."

His hands went behind his back and gripped each other as though they were a cliff's edge.

"But the truth is, I ignored anything that didn't further my business. The choices we make are the foundation of everything I care for, and yet I denied you the ability to make your own. I treated you well and told myself that meant I was good.

"I never dreamed I made myself part of something evil."

I struggled to find something to say. It was absurd, but I wanted to console him. He had treated me as property, however much worse he could have been. And yet I could not escape the desire. Could I tell him that I had been taught to expect constant abuse, and life here had had its joys?

Jon's hands unclasped, and he turned to face me in complete control of himself.

"I will not let you die, Chase." His voice was solid. "I will fight for your life. No matter what it takes."

He picked up his notebook and strode out of the room, his chin leading the way.

Shortly after he left, I began crying.

CHANGE

"Jon Galat, stodgy and stuck up as ever!" A laugh, full and deep, bellowed through the stones of the manor.

I knew that voice. I looked out the window, and there Delsaran was, his red hair flecked with grey. He strode up to Jon, who stood on the path to greet him.

Since our conversation, Jon had spent his time in his study, planning. And that morning he had dismissed all his staff and left us alone in his manor. Then, a few minutes ago, he told me to wait in his study, and he would join me shortly.

Even so, I had not expected this.

"Thank you for coming," Jon said. He gave a little bow.

Delsaran sauntered up to him. His short limbs swung wildly, and his body, thick with muscle and an exuberance for good food, swayed. "You must be pretty hard up to beg me for help." Delsaran laughed again, and slapped Jon's back.

Jon stumbled forward. He caught his footing and replied, "I am."

Delsaran froze mid-laugh and studied Jon. "I'm sorry for whatever happened. You've always been honest and flexible, even as I fought against you." He smiled again, but the mirth was gone.

Jon nodded. "I appreciate your kindness," he said. "You have consistently demonstrated your passion to protect those around you. Thus, I requested your presence today."

Delsaran chuckled. "Ah, the bureaucratic compliments of Jon Galat."

Jon smiled in his practiced way. "You are welcome to my home, Delsaran," Jon said. "I will provide anything I can to ensure your stay is comfortable."

"Come, then," Delsaran said. "Let's go inside." Delsaran placed his hand on the small of Jon's back, and guided him into his own manor.

Why would Jon invite Delsaran here? I wondered. Delsaran had fought Jon's business at every turn for years. He could fight, but if Jon needed a warrior, Avinna would have Delsaran at the point of her sword in a second. If Jon needed a negotiator, Marcus was every bit as good as Delsaran, and neither were as good as Jon.

By the time Jon opened the door and waved Delsaran into the room, no answer had come to me.

Delsaran saw me and smiled. "Good to see you, Chase."

I returned his smile as Jon had taught me.

Then Jon strolled past him and around the desk. "Please, sit," Jon said, motioning to the chair opposite his desk. His voice was gentle but commanding. Delsaran stared at him, then acquiesced and sat in the chair.

Jon sat and looked at Delsaran. "You reside in the woods a distance from Castulo, so I suspect you may not have heard the recent news."

"I haven't heard anything."

Jon nodded. "You have petitioned against my proposals while Chase stood beside me, and thus you are acquainted, correct?"

"I greeted Chase when I entered," Delsaran said.

"Of course," Jon said. He clasped his hands together on the desk and studied the curve of his finger. "He will be executed."

"What?!" Delsaran jumped to his feet and slammed his hands down on Jon's desk. "He's just a boy! How could anyone—"

"He is also a slave." Jon's voice pierced through Delsaran's yells.

"Scribbles on paper!" Delsaran bellowed. "People make decisions. No spirit is enchained to another but by force or choice."

"Unfortunately, there is a lot of force behind these words." Jon sighed. "He killed Rorvin."

"Valence's boy?"

"Indeed," Jon said, and then gave a quick description of what had happened since that night.

"Never trusted Valence," Delsaran said. "He only seemed to care about himself, not what was right."

"Or legal," Jon murmured in partial agreement. Then he spoke in his usual firm tones. "But he has cultivated power, and, legally, Chase has none." Jon placed his finger on the tip of his thin nose. "Even my connections have turned up nothing."

"You've beaten me more than I can count," Delsaran said. He glanced at the thick books that covered Jon's bookshelf. "I bet you know every detail of each book here. If you're giving up now, then you're not the man I thought you were."

"I would fight this until the rope is taught," Jon said quietly. Then he opened his mouth to continue and stopped himself.

I had never seen him doubt himself in a negotiation. Was my death that certain?

"But?" Delsaran asked.

Jon's fingers twitched. "I do not want to leave this to a judge."

"Jon Galat, doubting judicial oversight?"

"I understand the humor of the situation." Jon tilted his head, then spoke quietly. "I have never liked you, Delsaran. You are brash and impulsive. You leap into situations you know nothing about. And you always think of today, but never of tomorrow."

Jon leaned forward and stared into Delsaran. "However, more than any person I have ever known, you stand firm upon what you believe is right while Yryja herself rages against you. It is for that virtue I have called upon you today."

Delsaran had the glimmer of a smile. "Sincere praise from Jon Galat. What's next? Charity?"

"My life's work has been to further civilization," Jon said coolly. "I have invented new tools that make life and work easier and demonstrated to rulers near and far that wealth is made through trade, not war."

"And made yourself filthy rich while your labourers toil in squalor," Delsaran responded. "And destroyed the forests and mountains that nurture life and love."

Jon opened his mouth to retort, then brought his fingertips to his lips. He breathed and placed his hands back down on the desk. "I have a favour to ask of you," he said.

"If it's to save Chase, I'm in."

Jon's face remained perfectly still, but a few tears rolled down his cheeks, leaving the faintest trail until they disappeared into his thin lips.

"Thank you," he whispered.

Then Jon blinked, and his eyes had their usual penetrating gaze. And when he spoke, his voice was its usual steel. "I created a plan that can be put into effect immediately, pending your approval."

He lifted his hands and touched his index finger. "I have procured skeletal parts that match Chase's physique, some human, some bull." Middle finger. "All staff have vacated the premises for the night thanks to an anonymous patron who arranged for a free show of The Lord Provost's Players." Ring finger. "I have procured accelerant that will leave no trace, so the manor should burn down easily." Pinky finger. "Chase's bedroom is in the basement, so between the fire and falling debris, no one should be able to identify any dissimilarity between him and the skeleton—assuming anyone had even the slightest idea what to look for."

Delsaran chewed on his finger. "I like it," he said. "Drastic, but simple enough. I can't think of anything better." Delsaran looked over at me again. "But then what? Chase can't disguise himself, can't even move a town or two over. And there's no way he could come back."

"No, he would have to leave Castulo," Jon said. "That is the reason I need you."

Delsaran's eyes widened. "I understand," he said.

My breath caught in my throat. Leave Castulo? I did not want to die, but how could I abandon Bri?

"You will have to avoid paths and roads and live off the land," Jon said. "You will have to lead him to a safe place where he can live."

Delsaran nodded. "I didn't realise you trusted me so much."

Jon opened his arms, palms upward.

Delsaran gazed at me, and his eyes softened. He must have read my feelings in my face. I could not yet hide my emotions as Jon could.

"I'm sorry this is happening to you," Delsaran said. "It's wrong. And I wish I could make it all better. But I do look forward to getting to know you."

I appreciated his kindness, but his words did nothing to calm me. How could I tell him my heart yearned for Bri? *There are rewards from obedience*, I heard the slave-master say.

Delsaran's brow furrowed, then he looked back at Jon. "I said what I said, and I meant it—but I'll be gone for a long time. Who will fight for the forests? Who will keep the rivers running clear and the air crisp?" The corner of his mouth twitched, and his eyes shone. "Who will hold you to account?"

Jon smiled. He took a dossier from the side of his desk and opened it. Several pages, almost black with Jon's small, neat script, were bound together. He handed them to Delsaran, whose stubby fingers cradled.

"This is a proposal for a regulatory agency to protect our land and ecosystems, ensure workers are treated fairly, and monitor for examples of market failure." He paused. "And to allow no new slaves in Castulo."

Delsaran looked at the pages; his eyes glazed over.

Jon took another page out of the dossier: a ten-thousand gold piece bank draft from Eydora & Progeny. He tapped it with his index finger and said, "authenticate." The word activated the magic, and colours danced across the sheet's surface before forming the boar and the lion, the twin symbols of Eydora & Progeny. Then he placed it before Delsaran.

"Jon Galat," Delsaran said. He studied the bank draft. "I always knew you were honourable. But are you secretly good, too?"

"No," Jon whispered so low that Delsaran couldn't hear him.

Jon took a breath, then his voice rang out. "This money can go to any other cause you choose, of course. Even your own. But if you take my proposal, I guarantee that all my resources and influence with council will be devoted to this purpose."

Delsaran put the papers down. "It's too late to doubt you now. Let's do this." He held out his hand to Jon, and they shook. Their hands remained clasped for a moment after the handshake ended.

"I assume I leave tonight?" Delsaran asked.

"Yes," Jon responded. "I have been holding off the court for as long as I can."

My stomach sank, and I lost control. "Tonight? I can't even say good-bye?"

"Oh, Chase," Delsaran said. He embraced me. "I'm so sorry."

I sobbed. Tears ran into the fur that covered my face, matting it. I imagined Bri's smiling face, looking at me. *You want to be my sidekick?*

"Bri," I said, unable to say or understand more.

Delsaran glanced at Jon.

"The son of my bodyguards," Jon said. "About Chase's age."

"He's your friend, is he?" Delsaran asked.

I nodded.

"And you don't want to leave him? Don't want him to think you're dead?"

I nodded again.

Delsaran squeezed me tighter. He smelled of leaves. "I understand, lad. It's hard. But this must stay secret to work," he said. "Better for him to think you died than to see you killed by those who call you beast."

"He need not think you are gone forever, Chase," Jon whispered in a tone meant to be reassuring. "A few years from now, you can write him and tell him what happened."

I sniffled but said nothing. What could I say? How could I say it? I was trained to obey, not to fight for feelings I had been taught to deny.

And I knew the truth of what they said, too. If I were to live, Bri must think I were dead. I did not want to die. Therefore, I must accept it.

My body shook, and I cried.

What I understand now that I didn't then, is that there was something I feared so much more than mere death: being alone.

The negotiations done, Delsaran took me by my arm and led me outside and into the chill night. His fingers held me gently, but with constant pressure as we walked away from the manor. Still, I stopped to look back.

My eyes slid over the vaulted arch that was the ceiling of the great hall and the terracotta figurines that decorated the corners and spires of the manor. I peered through the dark until I could make out the silhouette of the forest behind the manor. In that forest, I had lain in the sun and told myself it was the same sun my mother looked into. In that forest, I played with Bri and found joy. In that forest, I had killed

Rorvin and changed my life.

Delsaran's grip grew firmer, and I knew I had to leave. But as I was about to turn, I saw Jon standing in the doorway. His back was to me, and his hand held the doorframe as though it alone stopped him from entering. I wondered if, like me, he paused for a sentimental moment about his manor, where he had lived since he had made his riches. It was his home, the symbol of his success, and must be the place of his joys.

Then he spoke. His voice was slow and soft, but the cool night air carried it well. He wanted to be sure I could hear.

"I have always known that evil people tortured and killed slaves," he said. "That's the way people work, I told myself: good people do good, and evil people do evil. And I—I have always tried to do good."

He let his head hang down. "I was a fool."

He turned, then stared me in the eye. There was a fierceness there, a wildness I had never seen in him before. "There will always be evil people, Chase. They see others as mere toys to be manipulated as they wish. Do not delude yourself that they do not exist, for that leads only to self-doubt while they plot your suffering.

"And there are great people, too. They have the humility to see where they have done wrong and the fortitude to set it right.

"But most people are like me, Chase. We do good in our way, but when the life we know is threatened, we care not who we trample to protect it."

His eyes lingered on mine for one last moment, then he turned and began to walk inside.

I barely heard his last words: "And thus we destroy those we love."

II

MORNING

"Good morning, Chase!" Delsaran bellowed. I shot up and found myself looking into his face. He grinned wildly, sitting on his haunches above me. "I made breakfast!" He thrust a bowl of berries, nuts, seeds, and roots toward my face.

I had had the same breakfast almost every day for the past three months. The first several mornings, I looked at it disdainfully, picking at the best-looking pieces to stave off the worst of my hunger. Even now, I could remember the flakey, buttery crusts of the pastries baked every morning in Jon's manor. But I had adapted to this foraged diet.

After all, I had adapted to much worse.

"You must have been slaving over the oven for hours!" I exclaimed with mock surprise. "Is it my birthday?"

Delsaran laughed, his belly shaking. "You're learning!" Then he scrunched up his face, as though he were thinking hard or constipated.

"Four out of ten," he said. "Could have used a bit more punch, and you went for the"—he tilted the bowl so it hung from his fingertips and the berries rolled around—"low-hanging fruit."

I laughed the same way Delsaran did, throwing my head back and letting my belly shake. But a lot of the mirth was faked, and he could see that. For Jon, I had applied myself to learn business and economics. For Delsaran, I applied myself to learn humour and banter.

I was better at the economics.

Still, he made me feel cared for in a way Jon never could. He regaled me with fantastic tales of magic and bravery throughout our journey.

Though even now I cannot say what parts of the stories were true and what were false.

I don't know if he could say, either.

That's not the point, lad! he had told me when I had finally worked up the nerve to ask him. *The point is the light it shines on your life!*

If I had had the courage, I would have responded, *And your words would shine a lot more light if I could trust a single one of them.* But as much as I knew he loved banter, that was still beyond me.

So, I grabbed the bowl from Delsaran's hand and thanked him sincerely. I ate while Delsaran stood and moved into the sunlight. He stripped naked and spread his arms as wide as they would go, as though he were trying to catch every ray of the sun. Then he recited his mantra:

"I open myself to your light,
    And you fill me.
I open my body to your warm caress,
    And you melt idle lethargy with joy and love.
I open my mind to your radiant serenity,
    And you bore through petty distractions with devotion.
I open my soul to your inferno,
    And you incinerate the stupor of self-doubt with passion.

"With the ecstasy of joy and love,
    I will nurture my fire.
With the clarity of devotion,
    I will carry my flame into the darkness.
With the resolve of passion,
    I will burn and bring light to the world."

He basked in the sun, his arms outstretched and his eyes closed. His grey and red chest hair glittered. Then he let his arms drop, and a small, content smile played across his face. Finally, he bent down to gather his clothes and dress himself.

The ritual finished, he said, "We'll arrive at Greenchapel today, Chase."

I nodded.

He gazed in the direction we were heading, smiling faintly. "I know the druid who founded the town, Andarta." He said the name with quiet reverence. "Ah, but she is beautiful. Not like the brittle charm of the cities, all makeup and frilly dresses, but a strong, resilient beauty, like a tree reaching for the sky.

"She wanted to explore, discover new plants, see the real world—beasts, monsters, and all. Build her home in the darkness and bring it light." Delsaran's eyes radiated joy and devotion. "She taught me my magic.

"There are few women I would marry, Chase, but I'd drop to one knee in an instant for her." He chuckled. "I used to watch her dig deep in the dirt for hours, then brush the hair out of her eyes, leaving smears of brown on her black skin.

"Of course, I never stood a chance with her. Not when I can grow a beard like this and piss standing up!" He roared and slapped my back.

Then Delsaran looked up at the morning sky. His voice was soft when he spoke again. "But I choose to celebrate what is. I have the respect and friendship of one of the most amazing people in the world, and I got to travel to Castulo and meet you. I'm happy.

Delsaran stood up. "Now it's time for your training."

I picked up my axe and held it fiercely as I thought of Bri.

A minotaur's got to have an axe.

"Show me the basic swings again, Chase," Delsaran said when we had found a suitable clearing.

I complied. I swung my axe across my body, putting my weight behind it, then let the momentum of the axe rotate my wrist. I twisted my hips, and the axe swung back. The axe's momentum carried my arm into the air, then I brought the axe down as a blur of silver and brown.

"Good," Delsaran said. "Good flow with your hips. Excellent speed and strength."

He thwacked my shield with his sword, and I almost fell over. "You forgot about your shield, though. An axe is balanced near the tip. That makes its blows stronger, but also less maneuverable. You've got to keep your shield in position at all times."

He smiled, but his voice was terse. "First rule of combat: don't die."

He put his hand on my shoulder. His voice was soft as he said, "Let's do it again."

I did the basic swings again, keeping my focus on my shield. It stayed up and ready as my body followed my axe.

"The swings were a bit weaker, but better that than dead." Delsaran put his sword on his shoulder. "Now do that a hundred more times. Engrave it into your muscles. You gotta keep that shield up even when you're swinging with all your might."

My axe and shield grew heavier with every swing until both felt like they were made entirely of lead. I couldn't imagine swinging my axe for hours through a pitched battle. Finally, I finished and collapsed on the ground.

Delsaran laughed and sat down beside me. "Good job, Chase. I know this land is hard. But a hard land is not a curse. It's a blessing. Greenchapel is a haven for those who felt the oppression of cities and kingdoms and wanted to build a new life on their own terms. There is no city guard, no court, and no authority beyond your voice and your axe. It's a poor village, but what good is wealth if it doesn't light the fire within you?

"That's the true sweetness of life, Chase: standing on your own two feet and shining bright like the sun."

Delsaran saw the face I had perfected for Jon's long speeches, part awe and part comprehension. "Don't pay too much attention to this doddering old man, Chase. Enough people have told you what to believe for a lifetime." He smiled. There was joy in it, but his eyes were sad. "When you find your passion, just remember that the sun's fire gives life to the world but feels no remorse for those who are too proud to find shade."

I felt the truth of Delsaran's words as I lay there, too tired to move. For all my skill in elocution and business, I had never felt more capable than here, knowing I could survive in these woods. I could forage and defend myself, now. I did not depend on anyone I didn't trust.

I imagined myself protecting Bri with my newfound strength. Living outside of society, where there was no slavery and no law. We could just be happy in each other's company. What else did I need?

And yet my mind recalled a speech of Jon's and impressed on me its equal truth.

Some think that the mere existence of wealth signifies moral standing. Idiots, all of them. Wealth simply signifies . . . money.

Some claim my wealth means I worked harder than everyone else. He laughed. *Absurd! I work in this plush study, with you to meet my every need. Meanwhile, my thousands of miners toil in sweat, soot, and darkness for twelve hours a day.*

Other people see my frail arms and claim my wealth means I stole from my workers. But just as I would die labouring in a mine, my miners would die in these thousand-page books, each dealing with a single law—and I must know fifty for a single transaction.

No one can do everything with the requisite skill. Short lifespans aside, our different interests, talents, and perspectives make us stronger together. Money just tells us which skills are rarest and most desired. He looked past me, as though he could see the whole world spread out before him.

Civilization alone turns individual interest and talent to the collective good.

Finally, my fingers were strong enough to pick up my axe. Wobbling, I stood and walked back to our camp. We packed up our things, and, as Delsaran turned to leave, I saw him look down, then crouch.

He reached out and touched a daisy reverently, its petals white and gleaming in the sun. I had seen thousands of them, yet his fingertips stroked its stem so softly that it scarcely bent.

With a deft twist of his hand, he picked it, then tucked it behind his ear. He kissed his fingers, and they glowed. He touched them to the broken stem of the daisy and whispered, "Thank you. Grow back strong."

The broken stem lengthened and formed a new bud. The bud grew larger, then blossomed, white petals opening to the sun.

He turned back to face me, his smile radiant. "Come, Chase," he said. "Let us enjoy this day together."

I smiled, and we walked off. I appreciated the kind words and the affection he showed me. Throughout these months, my lonely heart had latched onto him with love.

But each time he gazed into the sun, all I could imagine was Bri beside me, saying he knew my death was faked, and he had found me. We could adventure the way we always dreamed of. But as the day wore on, the dream faded, and I was left with a question I could not answer:

Would the hole in my heart ever be filled?

FAMILY

Delsaran pressed the back of his hand against my chest and stopped me. His foot hung in the air, frozen. I looked at him, confused, but he stared off into the distance.

"Greetings," he said to the empty air. "My name is Delsaran, and this is my companion, Chase."

I looked around, but saw nothing but the tall, thick trees that surrounded us.

"I lived in Greenchapel many years ago," Delsaran continued, turning slowly. "I am a friend of Andarta's."

I followed his gaze until I saw a vague shape striding towards us, maneuvering around tree and bush. A human figure, short and lithe, with a bow in one hand and a horn in the other, each held loosely by their side. Their skin was brown, and their features soft—though they had a hard, square jaw that reminded me of Delsaran.

"I hope I didn't spook you," they said. Their voice was light and gentle. "I'm Hayyan, and I use they and them as my pronouns. I'm from Greenchapel, as you guessed." They studied me openly, with a friendly curiosity.

"I'm guarding out here because—" Their head snapped to Delsaran. "You're Delsaran?" They scrutinized his grey and red beard, his short, stocky limbs, and his big hands. "Uncle Delsaran?"

Delsaran furrowed his brow. "What do you mean, *uncle?*" he asked. "I've never met you before. You wouldn't even have been born before I left. . . ." His eyes widened. "You're Andarta's child."

Hayyan nodded, and Delsaran laughed, deep and soft. "The magic worked!" He laughed again.

Hayyan dropped their bow and horn in the dirt and ran at Delsaran. He enveloped them in a massive hug, their lithe body swallowed up in his own.

"Mom always said I would get to meet you someday," they whispered into his chest.

"If I had known, I would have come back so much sooner." Delsaran squeezed them tight, then remembered I existed. He kept one arm draped over Hayyan as he turned to me.

"Chase, I'm sorry, you must be so lost. Hayyan is. . . my child." He smiled. "Andarta always wanted a family, so before I left Greenchapel she used magic to, well, have them." Delsaran grinned.

But I had been trained to meet people. "It is the greatest of honours to meet you, Hayyan," I said, and held out my hand to them.

Hayyan slipped out of Delsaran's arm and stepped toward me. They took my hand limply, their lips pressed together.

"Your father is noble and loving, a paragon of men," I said. "In a world of equivocation and hatred, he stands tall. I am privileged to meet his child."

Hayyan stepped back and their eyes glazed over. "What are you?" they asked.

I bowed, and intoned, "I am a minotaur from a far-off land, unseen before in Orachim, and perhaps never will be again."

Hayyan giggled, then stared at me awkwardly. "I'm sorry," they said, "I've never really had to do this before." They tried to emulate my tone. "I'm a human from Greenchapel." They looked down at their feet. "Never been anywhere else."

"I cannot wait to see Greenchapel," I said. "Delsaran has told me of the resilient people there."

"Can you use magic too?" Hayyan asked me. "I can't. Mom says I'm always too busy looking for something new, so I can't connect with what's around me."

"Alas, I cannot," I said. "But I am trained in negotiation, business administration, and economics."

"What's that?" Hayyan asked.

I did not know how to answer that question.

Delsaran chuckled. "Until a few months ago, he was a slave. Now, he's free, but he was forced to leave everything behind." Delsaran ruffled my hair. "He needs to find his own path."

Hayyan nodded. They looked almost like they had been reprimanded. "Sorry," they said.

"No apology necessary," I murmured.

"I only ask because mum always said that no one took to her magic as well as you did, uncle," Hayyan said.

Delsaran laughed. "Well, your mother's teachings have brought this old, tortured soul much joy. I was a broken man before I met her. She taught me how to open my heart again. And, Chase," Delsaran shouted, "she gave me a child!"

Delsaran pulled me and Hayyan into a giant hug and lifted us both off the ground.

He put us down, then spat out questions. "There's so much I need to learn about you! What do you do for fun? What were you like as a baby? What lights the fire in your belly?"

Hayyan's mouth hung open. A few words came out as they tried to answer all three questions at once, and they laughed.

After the laughter subsided, Hayyan spoke haltingly. "Well, I'm still looking for what lights the fire in my belly. For fun, I like reading about other lands. And you should ask my mom about what I was like as a child."

"So I should!" Delsaran exclaimed. "And she should be here for this! Is she in town?"

"Of course," Hayyan said without thinking. "She . . ." They closed their eyes tight, their face contorting. "You wouldn't know. No one has been able to leave safely for some time. It's why I've been set as watch."

Delsaran frowned. He put his hand in mine.

"Take us to Andarta."

"Delsaran," Andarta breathed. She sprang up from the dirt she had been digging in and ran. She barreled into him, her arms wide, then wrapped him into a hug and left a dirty smear on the back of his shirt. They smiled at each other like long lost lovers, though the passion in their touch was not sensual.

"I've missed you," she whispered into his ear, "and so has Greenchapel." She closed her eyes and squeezed him tighter. Her arms couldn't reach all the way around Delsaran, but she had a presence that made her feel his equal in size. Then she opened her eyes and noticed me.

I could see the streaks of dirt on her forehead, as Delsaran had mentioned, but I was unprepared for her eyes. They were gentle and fiery, joyous and passionate.

"And who are you, dear child?" she asked, breaking her embrace with Delsaran. Though not quite commanding, her voice was accustomed to compliance. "If you're a hugger, come let me give you a welcoming hug." She opened her arms.

I dutifully hugged her; she was warm and smelled of roots. I suspected there'd be dirt on the back of my shirt, too.

Then I introduced myself. "My name is Chase, dear Andarta of Greenchapel," I recited. "Delsaran has told me of your skill and determination, and I can see your beauty for myself." I bowed.

Andarta's eyes fluttered, then she laughed. It was a laugh like Delsaran's, deep and hearty.

I stood there awkwardly as Andarta's laugh subsided.

"You don't need to flatter me, Chase," she said. "You came with Delsaran, so you're already family." She put her hand under my muzzle and lifted my head gently.

"Instead, why don't you tell me your story? You seem a good, honest"—she examined my face, body, and horns—"boy, is it?" I nodded. "But something must have made you travel with that no-good rascal." She jerked her other thumb at Delsaran, chuckling.

"Hey!" Delsaran pouted. "Be gentle with me. I still haven't recovered from the great pancake catastrophe of 537." He turned down his bottom lip and gave us puppy-dog eyes.

"And you never will if I have anything to say about it," Andarta quipped back. Then she leaned toward me and whispered loudly, "It was awful. He tried to use his magic to aerate the pancakes—and turned them into bombs."

"A little more practice and they only would have exploded with flavour," Delsaran said. "Instead, I was banned from using magic in the kitchen for life."

"You're just lucky I hadn't taken a bite," Andarta said. "Then you wouldn't be here to complain about it." She grunted and crossed her arms. "He was cleaning pancake batter off the ceiling for weeks!" Andarta made a point of looking only at me.

Delsaran huffed. "At least I didn't discover a new gourd and end up pumping so much magic into its seeds that Greenchapel had nothing else to eat for a month!"

"Hey! My mistake was tasty," Andarta retorted.

"And," Delsaran said, glaring at her, "somewhat incompatible with the human digestive system."

Andarta narrowed her eyes at Delsaran. Then they both laughed.

"I've missed you," they said in unison.

I let out a breath I had been holding. I knew this was banter, but their mock-anger had made me afraid we would be kicked out of Greenchapel the day we arrived.

As her laughter subsided, Andarta turned to Hayyan. "You were on duty, yes?"

"Yes, mom,"

Andarta nodded. "Good." Then she thought for a moment. "As much as I would like to catch up with Delsaran, I'm sure he wants time with you. And I know you've asked me enough questions about him that you do too. Why don't you and Delsaran check with your mommy and mother to see if one of them can replace you as a guard."

Hayyan nodded, already grabbing Delsaran's hand and walking away.

But Delsaran stood still, smiling at Andarta. "Seems like congratulations are in order. Two wives and a child. You've built the big family you always wanted."

Andarta's eyes glistened. "I couldn't have done it without you, Del. Thank you."

"I expect to hear all the details of both of your weddings!" Delsaran said as he and Hayyan walked away.

Andarta watched them go before she turned to me. "I assume Delsaran told you about me, so why don't you tell me about yourself?"

"I am Chase Galat," I replied. "A minotaur from far overseas. Though

I may appear a beast, I am fluent in common, Dwarvish, and Sylvan. I have also learned the arts of negotiation, economics, and business administration."

Andarta laughed, though I heard a touch of sadness in it. "Is that what lights the fire in your belly?"

Delsaran had asked the same question. "I'm sorry, but I don't understand."

"What makes your body quiver with life?"

I stood, unmoving. How could I answer a question if I didn't know what the other person wanted to hear?

"What do you dream of?" she tried again.

I remembered Bri's smile as he asked me to be his sidekick. My stomach churned, but I could give no words to it.

Andarta studied my eyes, then said, "I suppose I've become a bit eccentric, living out here for so long." She tried so hard to sound sincere. "Let's go for a walk, and I will tell you the story of Greenchapel, for it is the story of many people's passions."

She picked up her staff from where it lay beside her, and we walked through the small village.

Greenchapel was an odd assortment of houses. Some were small and ramshackle; others were solid and wide. Some even looked half-built, as though the owner had grown bored and said, *Good enough.*

"We house those who had no home, or who needed to escape and find a new one where they could be themselves. So, we're all a bit odd here." She smiled. "And that includes me."

She looked down at my practiced listening face. "A girl broke my heart, and I needed to learn who I was without her. My original plan was to do that, then head back to the city."

She put her hand on my shoulder. "Instead, I built a home in these woods, digging up new plants, studying new animals, building a shelter, planting crops." She sighed contentedly. "I lost myself in each task . . . and found myself happier than I had ever been.

"Eventually, word travelled of the crazy lady living in the woods, digging up plants." She pointed to the house beside hers. It was one of the nicer houses in Greenchapel; by the fresh paint and decorated windows, I could tell the owner took pride in that. "That's when Twilight Dragon showed up," she said. "She's lived here for twenty-five years. She's a hard worker, a great cook, and eager to take care of whatever needs doing." Andarta tapped her fingers against my shoulder with each item she listed.

"Though she's not the type of person I would have expected to live here, not with a name like that. But I suspect her love of attention brought her here. She"—Andarta chuckled—"tends to be a passionate, if temperamental, lover.

"She needed some work to bury herself in, and I longed for companionship." Andarta laughed, quick and sharp. "Though if a man hadn't come along, I don't think she would have stayed much longer!"

Andarta moved down to the next house. "And that," she said, "is the house of—"

Three quick horn blasts pierced the air. Andarta froze. As the horn blasts repeated, Andarta turned her head back and forth, ensuring she heard their direction.

"It seems Greenchapel's history must wait." She looked at the axe and shield strapped to my back. "You know how to use those?"

I nodded.

"Then follow me, Chase, and stay behind me." She began running toward the source of those blasts. I followed.

"And if Delsaran didn't teach you," she shouted, "the first rule of combat is don't die!"

CONFLICT

The creature's body looked not like a physical object, but a void. I could only tell how far away it was by the grass its long, thin arms touched as it ran toward us. Yet, somehow, it glowed red. No matter how it turned, a red aura surrounded it from its blocky head to its stick-like legs. I could not make sense of it.

But I didn't give voice to my confusion—Andarta was busy. She clutched her staff tight as she kneeled. Her other hand glowed, and she pressed it against the ground.

Stalks of the long, thick grass grew and wrapped themselves around the creature's ankles. The creature managed to pull one leg free and stumble forward, but the grass snaked up its other leg and anchored it to the ground.

The creature tore at the stalks. Leaves erupted in flame, but strong green fibres grew back to fill each gap. They twisted under its knee, slid across its thigh, and wrapped around its hips. Then the stalks yanked the creature to the ground.

It lay flat on its belly, its oddly shaped limbs madly trying to shred the stalks binding it. Those limbs scarcely bent as it wriggled, swinging from the hip and shoulder, and they tapered down to nothing more than a point.

Andarta stood, her eyes never leaving the trees the creature had come from. "We call these nightbringers," she said. "Their bodies are a magic receptacle. Separate the smallest part, and their magic flows out, leaving them to dissolve into dust—though they will dissolve quicker from a severed head than an arm." Her eyes met mine, and her upper lip twitched. "Bigger hole."

Her hand stopped glowing, and she lifted it to motion at my axe. "Let's see how you use that thing," she said. "Cut off its head."

I lifted my axe; it felt heavier than normal. I tiptoed over to the nightbringer, watching every movement of its head and limbs. Could it communicate or attack, even while bound? I imagined its tongue shooting out and burning my hoof.

But, as I stood beside it, it just kept wriggling. *Rewards from obedience*, I heard the slave-master say.

I swung my axe and severed the head of the nightbringer. Specks of void-like black dust flowed out of the creature's body. They caught the wind and swirled around each other as they blew away.

"You know how to swing it," Andarta said. "That's good." She looked back to the treeline. "Everyone helps here, but you're too young to be on the front line. Are you skilled with a bow?"

I shook my head.

Andarta looked at a group of youth with bows, twiddling her fingers along her staff. "The best use of your axe is to guard the rest of the youth, then. They'll be firing arrows into the nightbringers, which releases some stored magic and slows them down. It won't kill them, but, when they reach us, we can handle them with . . . relative ease."

"Understood," I responded. I tried to imagine a horde of nightbringers, but could only remember the one I had beheaded, wriggling in the grass.

"We have learned to fight nightbringers well," Andarta said. She crouched low to the ground again, her hand pressed against the dirt. "Most will slam up against the front lines and be slaughtered by our fighters. But a few can slip around us. I'll appreciate someone there to watch Hayyan, and I know Delsaran will as well."

Her next words were loud and carried to everyone there. "We've probably got a minute and a half until the host arrives. Let's do this."

I walked past the villagers as they set up barricades out of logs, tables, and sheets of metal. They were flimsy and unsecured—but numerous. I counted four barricades, one after the other. So long as the nightbringers didn't circle around them, the villagers could keep retreating from one to the next.

Delsaran was at the first barricade. He watched the villagers with keen eyes, then aped them, constructing the barricades almost as fast as they did, though his arms moved with a nervous stiffness.

Delsaran noticed me watching him and smiled. "Don't worry about me, Chase! I may be old, and I may be slow, and my memory may be going, but I . . ." He looked at me, his eyes blank. "I seem to have forgotten what I was going to say.

"Have great hair! That's it!" He shook his head from side to side and his curly hair bounced. "And there is nothing more important in battle than looking good!"

I smiled, more from the effort he put into cheering me up than from what he had said. I could never understand how he found humour in covering latrines or fighting monsters. But Delsaran went back to work building the barrier and I, knowing my duty, turned and walked to the other youth.

"Chase," Hayyan said as I approached. They stared at me before extending their arm in greeting. We clasped arms just below the elbow.

They held the grip, then looked at my axe and shield. "Do you need a bow?"

I shook my head. "I would be useless with a bow," I said. Then I remembered the words I said to Bri, so long ago. "With my axe, I will protect you." I saw Bri's smile, and my heart ached for our adventures together.

"Oh, all right," Hayyan said. They let out a long breath and looked at the youth around us.

The youth shifted their weight from foot to foot, eyes darting across the clearing. But they held their bows with experienced hands. Hayyan's eyes lingered for a moment; I followed their gaze and saw deep scarring along the calf of one of their comrades. The boy favoured his other leg.

Hayyan turned back to me. "The nightbringers attack whatever's closest, so all the ones that come out of the forest head straight for the fighters in our gauntlet, but a few get turned around and come out behind us. If one does, let me know, and I'll make sure it's peppered with enough arrows that you can take it down easily."

I nodded. "I will watch your flank." Bri would be proud of me, I thought, and my heart swelled.

The twang of bowstrings brought me out of my reverie. I looked to the treeline, where a swarm of black shapes sprinted toward us.

The battle had started.

The villagers put the last pieces of the barricade in place. Some drew bows and moved to the flank while the rest drew an assortment of blades—swords, leaf-tipped spears, axes, sickles, and scythes—and moved behind the first barricade.

The nightbringers ran through the tall grass with long, loping strides. Andarta knelt and pressed her hand against the ground, and the branches at the treeline thickened, then grew into a dense web that caught the nightbringers—for a moment. They burned through branch after branch, and I worried that Andarta's magic was useless against them.

But as holes opened, the nightbringers squeezed through only a couple at a time. It wasn't designed to stop them but keep them manageable, I realised. Still, those that squeezed through her web sprinted toward the barricade.

A few looked utterly unnatural, limbs protruding from all over their bodies. Some ran on mismatched legs, their stride and body off-kilter. One had an arm that stuck straight up from its torso; its lump of a head protruded from its chest. Another had no arms at all, only little claws poking out from its hips.

Even with the fighters between us, I shook. I gripped my axe and shield, though I had no power to lift them.

The archers nocked their bows and fired. The arrows cut through the nightbringers before slamming into the ground.

The holes left by the arrows shone red so bright it almost hurt my eyes. Yet the nightbringers did not seem to slow. The ground beneath them disappeared step by loping step. Only after the second volley of arrows hit them did they slow, wafting through the air like clouds.

As the uninjured nightbringers swarmed past their now-slowed brethren, another round of arrows cut more bright red holes, and they slowed too. Now the fast, uninjured nightbringers breaking through Andarta's web clumped behind the slowed ones, unable to squeeze past. The next volley of arrows sailed right into these clumps, piercing through a handful at a time. The nightbringers continued to slow—but soon they would reach the barricade. I could only hope they had been slowed enough.

A last volley of arrows struck the nightbringers, then they crashed against the barricade. Their long, pointy arms strained to reach the soft flesh there.

But they were met with cold steel. The points of their arms were lopped off, and the first line of creatures disintegrated—but not before their remaining limbs attacked again.

Most were turned aside harmlessly, but one fighter cried out in pain. He dropped his sword, the skin on the back of his hand charred. He staggered back as the creature turned to dust.

Another nightbringer climbed over the barricade. The injured villager ran forward, reaching down with his off-hand to pick up his sword. The nightbringer groped for his chest, and the fighter swung his sword in an awkward circle to parry it.

The flat of his blade whacked the nightbringer's arm down, but not far enough. The nightbringer's arm dug into the fighter's thigh, and he screamed. His leg collapsed beneath him, and he crashed into the ground. The nightbringer approached him as more climbed over the barricade, their arms digging into the wood and steel.

The fighter scrambled back with his good arm and leg, but the nightbringer was still faster. It bent at the hip, its arm reaching down toward his face. The fighter's hand and foot scrabbled uselessly, slipping along the grass as he tried in vain to avert his own death.

Glowing white, Delsaran's sword sliced through the nightbringer's arm. It tried to bring its other arm to bear on the fighter, but Delsaran flicked his wrist and cut through the creature's torso, dispersing it in a second. Then he glanced at the nightbringers that climbed over the barricade and sprinted toward them, his sword shining brighter than their red auras.

One was over the barricade. Its arms reached for Delsaran. He swung through both of its arms, leaving its dust to settle on the ground.

Three more climbed the barricade, their limbs burning through the wood. Their arms groped for Delsaran as he approached.

At the last second, Delsaran leapt to his left, leaving the two on his right to flounder. The nightbringer on the left reached for him, but Delsaran cut through its arm, then whacked the creature with the flat of his glowing blade, sending it sprawling to the ground as it dissolved.

Delsaran faced the remaining two. Their pointy hands stretched for his head. Delsaran ducked beneath their arms and swung, slicing through their ankles. Delsaran dodged their last grope as they toppled, then blew away.

The defensive line restored, the rest of the fighters along the barricade spread out, making sure there were no gaps the nightbringers could get through. Andarta bent over the wounded fighter; she grabbed him by his armpits and hauled him back through the barricades, then bandaged his leg and hand quickly.

Andarta gave him some sort of leaf, and the man chewed it while she double-checked her knots, then touched her glowing hand to each bandage. Satisfied, she looked back to the line, searching for any other fighters that would need her aid. Seeing none, she kneeled and touched her glowing hand to the ground, and the stalks of grass that funneled the creatures toward the barricade grew taller and thicker.

Tempered, the line held. These villagers did not move with the practiced ease of armies in Castulo. But I could see the fire in each person's actions. I understood part of what Delsaran had told me about Greenchapel now. People here were not professionals who fought for money; they fought for themselves and their loved ones—because if they didn't, no one else would.

More nightbringers hacked through Andarta's web of overgrown branches and made their way into the clearing. Andarta sent more magic into the trees, trying to keep the nightbringers from swarming us. New branches grew across the gaps the creatures poured through, but the nightbringers broke through the growth before it could harden. The funnel widened.

"Get ready to fall back!" she shouted.

The archers moved back, firing a volley of arrows between each step. The fighters fought all the harder, keeping the nightbringers pinned against the barricade while the archers retreated.

Yet they could not hold the first barricade for much longer. The wooden planks had almost been charred beyond use, and the metal sheets buckled. Still, spears, axes, and swords all hacked through anything that poked over the barricade.

The wood failed first. A table burst into flames, forcing the fighter behind it to fall back. Not even Delsaran could hold against the flame, and the line bulged. The creatures flooded through the barricade, their bodies completely black as they ran through the fire.

"Now!" Andarta screamed. Her whole body glowed, and the grass along the barricade grew thick and tall, wrapping itself around the creatures' legs and feet. The fighters scampered back, sliding through holes in the second barricade and filling the gaps with metal sheets. Andarta's glow faded, and I could see her chest heave as she worked her way to her feet.

The creatures broke free of the grass and swarmed to the next barricade, where the fighters stood ready. The battle started anew.

But I had seen this fight now, so I was no longer entranced by it. I had a job to do.

I glanced around and saw three nightbringers coming at the youth from behind. They had probably been pushed out by the throng while the trees had been more intact.

Time to see if I could do more than just play as a protector.

"Three nightbringers over there!" I shouted, pointing at them with my axe. The youth turned, arrows already nocked. They drew and fired. The arrows tore through the creatures, leaving bright red holes. But the nightbringers kept coming.

"Chase!" Hayyan shouted over the din off battle, "I'll help you fight them off."

A flash of white caught my eye from the barricades. I looked back, and Delsaran sliced through a line of them, his sword blazing. He wrapped his other arm around a wounded fighter; one of her arms hung limply while her other awkwardly swung her spear from side to side. Delsaran pulled her back, his sword chopping through arms that got too close.

Andarta lumbered toward them. I looked to the treeline and saw that almost all her web had been burned away, and the nightbringers rushed through.

Delsaran put the fighter down and sprinted toward the line. He moved faster than I had ever seen him, his sword a blur of light. Arrows flew over his shoulders as the archers desperately tried to keep up with the mass of nightbringers.

Andarta knelt over the fallen fighter, her hands glowing. One touched the fighter's wounded arm while the other pressed against the ground, trying to strengthen the trees. With her attention split, the nightbringers burned through the web as fast as it regrew.

Those fighters needed all the support they could get. I had done this with Bri a million times. I knew what I was supposed to do.

"No," I said, "your job is to slow that horde. The fighters are counting on you." I stepped toward the three nightbringers coming toward us. "I will protect you."

The words felt good to say, but I immediately cursed myself. Would one fewer archer have made a difference in their battle? I had merely sparred with Delsaran and play-fought with Bri before. Could I actually fight?

Experienced fighters had gone down from a single blow of those sharp arms. And as the closest nightbringer advanced, step by plodding step, it lifted its long, spindly arms. It reached toward me as though it could will its arm longer. It was a thing of death.

And I had stepped into its path, alone.

I wanted to shout at Hayyan to come help, but I couldn't open my muzzle to say the words. Instead, I whispered what Delsaran had told me: "First rule of combat: don't die."

I considered swinging my axe at the nightbringer as it approached, hacking off its arm like all the fighters had at the barricade, but I didn't have their experience. If I swung too early, I would miss and leave myself open. If I swung too late, it could hit me even as I sliced through it.

Instead, I stood there as its long pointy arm touched my shield. It screeched against the metal, deafening me.

"First rule of combat: don't die," I told myself, unable to hear my own words. I slammed my shield into its arm, knocking it away. Its shoulder fell back, and the creature twisted; its other arm swung toward me.

I jumped back just as its arm passed in front of my face. My eyes and skin burned. I could see nothing but that intense red light—and then darkness.

I blinked several times. I could just make out the glowing fringe of the creature, its torso twisted away from me. It started to turn back, but this was my chance.

I swung my axe, careful to keep my shield in place, praying to whoever would accept my plea that my axe would strike true.

My axe hit the nightbringer's side and sliced clean through its torso. The nightbringer vanished almost instantly, black flecks flying into the air, carried off by the wind.

My breath came in little gasps. My aching fingers clenched my axe's haft.

I had killed a nightbringer.

But the two remaining nightbringers ambled toward me, side by side. One was like the rest, long-limbed and sharp. The other was even less human, a single short arm sticking out of its forehead. Long-arm and head-arm, I named them.

How could I fight them both?

I could try to hack through them both at once. If I could pull it off, I'd win the battle in a single blow. The quick plan.

Long-arm was more dangerous. If I could take it out quickly, I'd be able to destroy head-arm with relative ease. The middle plan.

Head-arm was less dangerous. If I killed it first, I could battle long-arm with less risk. The safe plan.

The nightbringers were almost upon me. I repeated Delsaran's words to myself and decided I'd go with the safe plan.

I circled around the nightbringers until long-arm was right behind head-arm. Long-arm reached for me over the shoulders of head-arm, but that gave me some space. I judged my distance to head-arm and readied myself. If I missed, they could both attack me at once. I had to get this right.

I waited, each second harder than the last. My arm twitched. My pulse beat against the shaft of my axe. My breath came fast. Head-arm took a slow step. I repeated Delsaran's words. Head-arm took another step.

I swung. My axe sailed toward its hand—and passed just in front of it. My axe continued across my body. I let my wrist roll over; the axe head circled around, and my muscles tensed to strike back.

But head-arm took another step, and its hand struck my shield. The metal squealed as the shield shook. I couldn't push back this time—I was still recovering from my missed swing.

Head-arm drove me back. I tried to keep my balance, but swung my axe high into the air, missing the nightbringer completely. I kept it against my shield but couldn't get my footing to attack it. I had to kill it before long-arm could reach me. . . .

But long-arm was already there. It groped toward me, and I had to turn my shield against it. I tried to brace my shield for the blow, but my whole body shivered as the metal whined.

I swung my axe again, but they pushed my shield into me, and my hooves slid along the grass. My swing turned into a helpless flail. Off balance, my shield fell away; head-arm reached right for my heart, its black-red point coming closer.

I swung my axe wildly while head-arm brushed against my chest; it burned through my shirt and seared my flesh.

Then the haft of my axe came down and knocked it away. I got my hooves under me and leapt back, finally getting some space between me and the nightbringers.

I tried to circle around them like before and swing at one while the other was behind it, but the nightbringers were too close to the other youth now. Long-arm turned to face me, but head-arm kept loping toward the youth.

I had promised to protect them. I ran between the nightbringers and the youth and let the nightbringers come toward me.

I glanced back at the young archers I protected. My battle had carried me behind them; they wouldn't see me struggle if I were wounded. The second barricade had been destroyed, and the fighters had pulled back to the third. Its chairs and tables looked charred and ready to give way, and there was only one more barricade for them to fall back to.

I couldn't get help. All my life, I had done whatever was needed to survive. Now, I faced death alone.

I had to do something fast, yet my arms already sagged, my axe and shield heavy. I breathed and let the swell of panic wash over me, then float away. The only thing that mattered was survival. How could I attack one without my guard dropping for the other?

Head-arm could bend from its torso, but it was slow to do so, I realised. I could get in close and hack at its legs.

My one advantage, my range, would be gone. But I was running out of space anyway.

My arms burned and my legs quivered as the nightbringers took one long, slow loping stride forward. The red light that fringed them took up more and more of my vision. Long-arm's hands screeched along my shield, and I planted my hooves against its push.

As head-arm's hand stretched for my face, I fell to my knees. I held my shield against long-arm as head-arm bent at the hip, reaching for my flesh.

I swung.

My axe cleaved through its legs, and head-arm toppled. It landed on its side, the tip of its arm reaching for me even as it dissolved into black flecks and blew away.

Long-arm still pressed against my shield, so I leaned into it, pushing long-arm back like I had the first nightbringer. There was a moment's resistance—and then nothing. I almost toppled into where the creature had to be. How could there be no resistance?

Then I saw them—the black and red arms had reached around my shield and groped for my face.

I fell onto my ass and the hands passed right in front of me. I crab walked backwards, but my axe and shield dragged on the ground, and I couldn't get the space to climb back to my feet. Long-arm was slow, but I was slower.

I stopped trying to move and let my ass hit the ground again. I was not going to get away—not with my weapon intact. My only chance was to strike now. And not miss.

I willed myself to keep my eyes open, but closed them anyway, and I swung, my arms barely able to lift my axe.

My axe hit long-arm and cut into its flesh—but my arms gave out mid-swing and my axe stopped. I tried to pull my axe clear, but I didn't have the strength. It stayed stuck, and long-arm reached for me.

Panicking, I rolled over my arm, hoping the weight of my body would be enough. My axe quivered, then sliced through; the axe head buried deep into the ground.

Lying on my belly, I felt the heat of long-arm on my back. It burned, and I cried in agony—and then it was gone.

My breaths came shallow and hard. My heart beat faster than I thought it could. I tasted dirt in my muzzle. Every muscle in my body ached. I smelled the seared flesh from my chest and back.

But I had survived.

RESOLUTION

By the time I had the strength to look up, the battle was almost over. Though the fighters had been pushed back to the last barricade, that barricade was intact, and no new nightbringers streamed out of the woods. The archers fired a last volley of arrows, then lowered their bows as the remaining nightbringers engaged the fighters.

I lay there as the fighters hacked the nightbringers into dust. I thought vaguely that I should get up, but the thought had no power to move my leaden body.

"Chase," a nearby voice said. I turned my head and recognised Hayyan. "You all right?"

"I am fine," I said habitually.

Hayyan started to laugh but then their eyes went to my back. "Krek, Chase," they said.

They kneeled over me and brushed their delicate hands over my fur. "You lost a lot of fur. Your skin blistered, but it's intact."

I nodded.

Hayyan looked back toward the barricade. Everyone patched up each other's cuts and burns while Andarta examined those she had pulled from the battle. She checked their ears and head for fluid before tightening her knots and tapping the bandages with a glowing hand. Then, for those who could not walk, she directed others to carry them back to the village.

"I would have come in a second, you know," Hayyan said. "We protect each other here. And that means you, too." They smiled and offered me their hand, but I waved it off.

I tried to lift my chest off the ground, but my arms gave out. I collapsed and fought back bile. I rested for another moment, then slid onto my knees.

I swayed slightly as I caught my breath. Finally, I stood, and was ready to speak. "Your job was to slow them," I said. "My job was to protect you from them." The simplicity of my words belied the anger and terror I had felt facing those creatures alone. But Hayyan was only trying to help.

"Chase," Hayyan said, "I just do what needs doing."

I had heard Delsaran say the same. Jon, of course, said the opposite: *How many pins could a recluse make in a day? One? Two? He scoffed. Give me ten workers and a factory, and I will make forty-eight thousand.*

Of course, I need civilization to provide their other needs, build the factory, and sell the pins. But in needing others, I make them richer, too. Those who live as hermits, scraping by with tooth and nail, diminish not only their own wealth, but that of the whole world.

Jon's speech had seemed true then—and still did. That was the path to prosperity, I knew. And yet, I felt something inside me that Jon had not prepared me for. Something that burned . . .

Most people with Jon's power take fairness as an insult, Delsaran had said as we journeyed to Greenchapel. *Jon sees everyone as a chess piece, yes, but he sees himself as just another pawn to be sacrificed on the altar of progress. Through his effort, future generations have better medicine, more food, less work. All the numbers go up.*

But we have lived in this wilderness for months now, Chase. Have we starved? Have we sickened? Have we been unhappy?

I had squeezed myself against Delsaran, then. He reeked of sweat, but felt so warm, and I was at peace.

When you protect the people you care about with nothing but your own strength, and you triumph . . . you'll feel the fire burn in your belly.

I understood Delsaran's words now. For every part of me that was still terrified of the nightbringers, still angry that I had been left to fight them, and still embarrassed that I had not asked for help, there were ten parts of me that wanted the creatures to come back tomorrow. I would fight them all over again.

And triumph.

"Chase! Hayyan!" Delsaran's voice boomed across the field. He shuffled as fast as he could toward us. The point of his sword trailed along the ground by his side.

As he approached, he saw that we were unharmed, and he smiled. He dropped his sword and lumbered over to Hayyan. He wrapped them in his arms and hugged them tight.

"Hayyan," he said, "your arrows were amazing. When I first saw those things coming toward us, fast and red, I didn't know how we'd stand against them. But your arrows slowed them to a crawl and made them easy prey."

Then Delsaran hugged me. My raw back ached as his big hands clasped it, but I still welcomed his touch. "Chase," he said, "Andarta told me she put you in charge of guarding the youth. I knew they would be safe in your hands."

"Chase took out three of them," Hayyan said. "Told me not to help so that I could keep firing arrows."

"Three by yourself? That's my boy!" Delsaran laughed. "I know how hard you trained all those months we were traveling."

Delsaran's hug slackened, then he reached out with one arm and pulled Hayyan into the hug. "This is my family," he said. "The brave child I always wanted but didn't know I had, and the son who grew through hardship to become worthy of respect. I love you both with all my heart."

A laugh erupted from my chest, catching me off-guard, and my whole body shook with it. I held Delsaran and Hayyan with all my might and whispered it to myself: "My family."

Delsaran stroked my back softly. His fingers brushed my fur, checking the skin as Hayyan had. "Life here will not be easy, Chase. But you have a home now."

Delsaran kissed me on the top of my head.

"And Hayyan," Delsaran continued, "We have only met today, but you have showed me your strength, your determination, and your heart. I couldn't be prouder."

The hug might have lasted forever if Andarta hadn't started laughing at us. "I see Delsaran is as sappy as ever," she said.

"Guilty as charged," Delsaran said. "A man who's afraid to cry is a man who's afraid to live."

"You're one to talk, Mom," Hayyan said. "You do the same thing every morning." Despite their words, Hayyan squirmed out of the hug.

Andarta smiled and held up her hands. "I can't help it if the chair of the village council demanded ten minutes of hugging a day. I have to set an example." She looked at me with a twinkle in her eye. "The fact that I am the chair is immaterial."

Hayyan snorted.

Delsaran squeezed me a final time, then released the hug. "I take it these creatures are why you had guards in the forest?" Delsaran asked.

"Yes," Andarta responded. "I should have told you. I was so happy to see you that I didn't—"

"Not your fault," Delsaran said. "Hayyan told me something was wrong. That's why we sought you out. Then I saw you and forgot everything else." Delsaran sighed.

"Fighting nightbringers has become a way of life for us," she said. "We just haven't been able to stop them."

"Sounds like you need someone who can track down their source," Delsaran said. He picked up his sword and examined the blade for nicks.

"Thankfully, a big strapping man came to town recently." Andarta blinked with exaggerated flirtatiousness. "I saw him slay so many of the nightbringers with his manly strength."

"Mom!" Hayyan said, even as Delsaran puffed out his chest and opened his mouth to speak.

"And he has such gorgeous horns!" Andarta finished, turning to me, her arms wide.

Delsaran sputtered in mock rage. My shoulders relaxed and my belly shook as I laughed.

"Look," Delsaran pouted, "Chase may be the hero, but I'm the one who taught him." He crossed his arms and lifted his shoulders. "I deserve some credit."

"I suppose ancient knowledge is good for something," Andarta whispered in a voice that would have carried to Castulo. Then, with a grand curtsey, she turned to Delsaran and said, "The Village of Greenchapel is forevermore indebted to you, Sir Del, for imparting the skill of the elders to someone who can actually fight."

Delsaran's jaw dropped, and his eyebrows slanted. "Well, I—"

"Now now, mom," Hayyan said. "Don't be too mean to my great-uncle. After all, it's heroic for him to get out of bed in the morning."

Delsaran clutched his chest.

I pushed down a well of anxiety, and said, in my most dignified, Jon-like voice, "I will speak well of you in my autobiography."

Delsaran's head whipped around to face me, his eyes crinkling. "You too, Chase?" he said, then he fell onto his back, letting the long grass envelop him. "Leave me here to die. I have lived my life and passed on what I could. Remember me fondly, Chase and Hayyan." Then his voice turned hard. "And remember that Andarta will belong here shortly!"

Andarta's laugh fluttered across the grass, and my heart swelled. And though I still felt the lack of Bri—and even Jon—there was only one word that filled my mind and body:

Family.

GROWTH

When we had recovered from the battle, Andarta gathered me, Delsaran, and Hayyan together in her home. It was a small home, and the only decorations were trees grown into remarkably expressive statues; the curved trunks twirled as though they were frozen mid-dance.

A table filled the middle of the room. Hayyan set out tea around it, and we sat.

"You need to know everything we've found out about the nightbringers if you're hunting them," Andarta said. "Unfortunately, nightbringers are creatures of arcane, bookworm magic, and most of that is beyond me."

She didn't say *bookworm* with disdain, exactly. I could hear the respect and awe in her voice. But there was something else, too. Some incredulity that a person would shut the world out to sit in a parlor, study books, and master them. Whether arcane magic—or law and economics.

"Have you tried tracking them?" Delsaran asked.

"Of course," Andarta said. "But they wander around the forests, following whatever animals they come across. They circle over so many tracks—including their own—that we eventually lose them and have to turn back."

Delsaran nodded. "What else have you figured out?"

Andarta pursed her lips. "They have no purpose."

"No purpose?" Delsaran leaned forward, his words sharp. "These nightbringers took a lot of magic to create. Why would someone go to that much trouble if they didn't have a goal?"

Andarta smiled. "Come now, Del. How many mages have we met who are just smart enough to figure out how to summon ancient, nameless demons, but not quite smart enough to figure out you should *never do that?*"

"True, true," Delsaran laughed, but then the sharp voice came back. "But this has been going on for over a year now." He let his words sink in. "Someone is maintaining them."

"Some*thing* must be maintaining them. Not necessarily some*one.*" Andarta leaned back and crossed her arms.

"Point for Andarta," Delsaran said, holding up his hands. "But you still haven't convinced me."

"How can I when you keep interrupting me?" Andarta asked with a melodic lilt. Then the playfulness dropped from her body, and she held her hand in the air, shaped in a fist. "There are three main reasons I think the nightbringers are without purpose."

She lifted one finger. "They have no goal in their destruction. They wander around and attack aimlessly. They're as happy to destroy a beaver dam as Greenchapel."

She lifted her second finger. "The creatures themselves are not meant for battle. They are powerful and burn through flesh, yes. But they are mere bottled magic, easily dispersed, and slowed by arrows. Using less magic, golems would deflect arrows and swords alike and have the strength to kill us in a single blow."

She lifted her third finger. "They are tactically clueless. Even now, with all we learned, if two groups attacked at the same time, it'd be over."

She crossed her arms and leaned back in her chair, her eyes glowing with triumph. "And so, these nightbringers were an accident, a product of a mage whose vision and intellect exceeded their wisdom and control."

Delsaran stroked his beard. "And you're certain they could have no goal?"

She groaned, then looked across the table at me and Hayyan. "This is how he always starts when he thinks he has me, the Yryja-cursed fool."

She turned back to Delsaran. "No goal makes sense. Terror? Maybe at first, void-like and glowing red. But now? We're careful, but not scared. Rampant destruction? Coordination would allow them to destroy us much easier. Containment?" She snorted. "We've done more exploring since this started, trying to find out where the Krek they come from."

Delsaran crossed his arms and leaned back. "What if they didn't know Greenchapel existed?" he asked. "An army of them would destroy us, true, but any three-town kingdom can raise a bigger army with its own mage. And a nightbringer army would leave a clear trail back to its source. But tracking down thousands of independent groups that just react to whatever they see? Impossible. And defending against constant, unpredictable assaults is exhausting and expensive.

"Guerilla warfare at its finest."

Andarta glared at Delsaran, her eyes burning with hate, then she laughed. "Oh, Del, I have missed you. No one else is willing to play Tigas." She smirked. "Though I do sometimes wish it didn't come quite so naturally to you."

Andarta's smile faltered. "But if you're right, it makes finding the source of this much more dangerous."

Hayyan bolted upright, spilling tea on the table.

"I'll be fine," Delsaran said. "I always am, don't worry." He looked over at me. "And I'll have Chase with me!"

"Of course!" I answered before I even knew what I had agreed to.

"That's my boy," Delsaran shouted.

My heart felt ready to burst.

He turned back to Andarta, though his eyes lingered on Hayyan for a moment. "So, we'll be fine. There's no need to worry."

She leaned over the table and kissed him on his cheek. "Thank you, Del."

"Can I go with them, mom?" Hayyan asked.

Andarta scratched her chin. "You lead the other youth. That's not a job we can just replace."

Hayyan's hands clenched.

"I know you want to explore the world," Andarta continued, "but they'll just be marching through the same woods you grew up in."

"I could hear about how Chase and Delsaran lived," Hayyan said.

"What Castulo is like."

"And you will," Andarta said. "But Chase and Delsaran will rely on stealth and speed. Whether two or three face a horde, the result is the same. But without you to lead the youth, the next horde that comes to Greenchapel could be the last."

"I won't be staying here forever," Delsaran added. "You can come with me when I go, and we'll explore the world together."

"It's always later," Hayyan said. They stood, their chair skidding out behind them, then stormed out of the house. We all stared at the door as it closed behind them.

"I'm sorry, love," Andarta said to the door.

After a long moment, Andarta coughed, then said, "I don't have anything more to offer you. I don't know how to defeat them for good. In the end, I've failed to stop them, and I'm relying on you once again, Del."

Delsaran held her hand. "You've put everything you have into protecting Greenchapel. That is nothing to be ashamed of. There's no point stopping the nightbringers if you lose everything doing it." Delsaran's voice was soft and smooth. "You are a wonderful leader."

Andarta nodded. She held his hand tighter as he spoke, but there was a hardness in her eyes that Delsaran missed. "I know." Her voice quivered like a struck steel blade. "It just makes your job harder."

Delsaran laughed. "Don't you worry about us. We'll return heroes!" He slapped me on the back.

Andarta looked at me. "You're going to need some better equipment. That axe of yours—"

"Chase left his old home in a hurry," Delsaran said, his voice low.

"Right." Andarta nodded. "So, new axe. And we'll have to get you some armour. Your shield protected you well, but a breastplate could turn aside a hand that gets past it."

Delsaran nodded, and then, in a voice more plaintive than I was used to hearing from him, said, "And I'd like more time with Hayyan, before we go." He looked down. "If they'll talk to me."

Andarta nodded. "They will. They've just wanted to leave Greenchapel for a long time. And I was going to take them, but then the nightbringers came, and . . ."

"I understand," Delsaran said, squeezing her hand.

"Give Hayyan a few minutes to cool down, then you'll likely find them under the giant redwood," Andarta said. "I'll help size Chase for his armor and weapons."

"I'd like to use my magic to help smith them," Delsaran said. "He's my boy, after all." Delsaran rubbed my head and smiled at me the same way Bri had, so long ago.

I would follow him to the ends of the Earth.

A few days later, Delsaran came to me, axe in hand. "You won't find a better-forged weapon outside a royal smithy," he said.

Its head glittered in the sunlight. I closed my hands around its shaft and marveled at the smoothness of the wood.

"I can't enchant—I don't have that kind of magic. But I purified and tempered the metal, and made the wood grow straight and strong along the grain."

"It's beautiful," I said. Then I remembered that Andarta had said something similar about her magic. "What kind of magic do you have? I read that mages understand the laws that govern the world and apply their will to change them exactly where they want. But that's not your kind."

"It's not one I would be good at." He chuckled. "I have the will but lack the intellect. I can't cut to the core of an idea the way Jon does."

Delsaran held his hands over his heart. "But the only facts that matter are in here." He smiled. "This is where we have chosen to be. Sometimes, the only options are bad ones. And, sometimes, people force our choice with swords or laws. But in the end, we still choose— no matter the consequences.

"Accept those consequences without reproach, and you can love every piece of this world, no matter how painful. Feel the sun's heat. Listen to the birds in the trees. Taste the air in your mouth. Smell the wet grass. Let them flow through you and love them with everything you have: the world, these people, this place. Take them inside of you, make them part of you. Then—choose."

I tried to imagine that. I had felt love before, with Bri, Delsaran, and Hayyan. But even as I thought of Bri, my heart ached. How could I love that which tore me from him? I had had no choice but to leave. Choice had been taken from me all my life.

Delsaran saw the frustration on my face. "It is not for everyone," he said, his voice deep and gentle. "And when something is beyond our experience, words are mere shadows of its essence. Perhaps, someday, you will feel something—and suddenly these words will make sense. Or perhaps not."

Delsaran held me. "I do not know what is right for you, Chase. But I have seen your strength, and your heart. You will accomplish much, whatever you do. I am certain of that."

I hugged him and felt the warmth of his body. His heart beat in his chest, slow and strong.

"I prepared these as a special surprise for you," Andarta said as we walked toward the edge of Greenchapel. She and Hayyan had come to see us off as we left to track down the nightbringers' source.

Andarta held out both her hands. One grasped the top of a bag small enough to fit in our packs; her other hand held a few golden wedges of what I guessed was food of some kind.

"I found these tubers a few years ago and used my magic to make them more nutritious and delicious. Now, a piece the size of your palm is good enough for a meal." She popped one in her mouth. "And they taste especially good fried."

I took a piece and tried it. The flesh was crisp as I bit into it, but tender and velvety beneath. Savoury and salty, with a hint of sweetness, it was delicious. "That is really good, thank you," I said. "Does it have a name?"

Andarta shook her head as she gave a piece to Delsaran. "I must confess I'm bad with names."

I thought for a moment. *Get a name that sticks in people's heads, and your product is halfway sold,* Jon had said. "How about Tubelicious? Because it's a tuber, and too delicious."

Andarta laughed. "I love it! I'm going to go tell everyone. They'll hate me so much."

She gave me the bag, and I put it in my pack. Then we were ready to go.

Andarta gave Delsaran a hug, and I did the same to Hayyan.

"You'll have to tell me more about Castulo when you get back," they said as I held them.

"I promise."

"Del," Andarta said. "Thank you for coming back and"—she chuckled—"going off again."

"Always," Delsaran said.

We broke the hugs, then Hayyan and Andarta switched places. I hugged Andarta while Hayyan hugged Delsaran.

"Take care of Del, Chase," Andarta said. "But don't forget to find yourself, too."

"I will."

"I love you, uncle," Hayyan said, "but I will hold you to your promise."

"As soon as Chase and I return triumphant," Delsaran said, "we'll explore the world together."

Our goodbyes said, we separated, and turned to leave.

As we started walking out of Greenchapel, I remembered leaving Jon's manor. I was so lonely then, stripped of the only people I had ever known, and the only place I remembered living.

I did not feel lonely now. I was scared, I knew. Part of me wanted to simply lie in the grass and look up at the same sun my mom did, with Delsaran, Hayyan, Bri, and even Jon by my side. I didn't want to go back into the wilderness where I would eat foraged fruit and nuts, wipe with leaves, and sleep on rough ground while dreaming of a void-black limb that glowed red.

As we reached the forest, I looked back at Greenchapel. I had not been there long. Aside from Andarta and Hayyan, I had met few of the people who lived there. Even Andarta's two wives were no more than names to me.

And yet, I thought of Delsaran holding me and Hayyan tight. I thought of Andarta digging in the dirt. I thought of my triumphant battle over the nightbringers, and Hayyan's gratitude.

This place was important to me.

I had spent most of my life helping because it was expected—and enforced. Delsaran wanted me to come, so I would. My own feelings were irrelevant. But now that I was leaving, I found myself saying that I would find the nightbringers' source and stop it.

I didn't know what to call the feeling. I searched for a word that captured the belonging and acceptance and love, and the drive to keep it safe.

Home.

I would protect my home.

III

ADVENTURE

We trudged through the wide river, holding our packs, clothes, and armor above the water. I shivered, most of my warmth pulled downstream by the current. Delsaran hummed as if he were in a warm bath, though I now knew what will and training that took.

I scanned the far side of the river, hoping to find any trace of the nightbringers. For the past two years, we had followed trails for weeks, sometimes months, and their tracks would disappear somewhere like this river. In the end, we would head back to Greenchapel to resupply and shelter through winter.

Finally, we reached the bank. I shook my fur while Delsaran's hand sluiced the water off his body. We let the sun warm us for a while, then dressed and searched the riverbank.

There were rarely any marks on the ground to follow. The nightbringer's legs seemed to leave grass unbroken, as though they had almost no weight at all. But the nightbringers would swipe at any critter they saw, leaving huge clefts in the trees. Or a dead carcass. It was unreliable, but the best way we had to track them.

"You go down that way." Delsaran pointed downstream, where the river bent and was lost among the trees. "I'll go this way." Delsaran pointed upstream, where the river's blue water broke white on jagged rocks.

Delsaran always took the harder way. And, since we had walked downstream to cross the river, it was also the way more likely to find them.

I smiled as he always did, trying to show enthusiasm for the task. "Will do," I said.

Then, as I was about to turn away, Delsaran said, "Oh, and Chase?" He grinned. "You know why Jon always throws coins into the river?"

"Why?" I asked.

"Because he loves studying his cash flow." He laughed, deep and hearty. Then he winked at me and walked away, one arm raised above his head in a parting wave.

I laughed for him, the sound high in my tight chest and throat.

Would we find a cleft in a tree? Maybe. But we'd lose it again. I would just have to put up with it and try to take what pleasure I could.

When we first left Greenchapel, I had connected with something living deep inside me. But now, when I remembered Delsaran saying that I had to embrace my choice and love where I was, I just felt . . . depressed.

I breathed and reminded myself I was not the boy I had been. I did want to protect Greenchapel. It was still home. I had found a family with Delsaran and Hayyan, no matter how I missed Bri.

And yet, after empty forests and vacant meadows, after barren hills and frigid rivers, after sleeping on rough dirt and foraging for food, I had deadened myself to the world. Delsaran tried to keep my spirits up, but I had spent a lifetime learning to suffer without complaint in the hope that someday, somehow, I would receive a moment of happiness.

"There is nowhere I'd rather be than here," I lied as I saw yet another tree without any gouges. Every part of my body ached. If we lost this trail, it would be time to head back to Greenchapel to resupply. I almost hoped we did lose it—then I'd be able to sleep in a bed and eat real food.

I breathed in, held it, and let it out. Maybe I should ask Delsaran how he loves so strongly, I thought. It was almost time to turn around and head back upstream, anyway.

Nightbringers wouldn't walk this far through a curving river unless they were chasing a big animal. But a big animal couldn't climb the river's jagged rocks, and if it had moved to land, there would be gouges through the trees as the nightbringers hunted it.

I picked up a rock from the side of the river and skipped it along the water. It hopped three times, then plopped beneath the surface. "One more bend," I said to myself, then continued walking.

I rounded the bend, and—nothing. No marks on the trees, no animals, not even birdsong. Just the oppressive stillness of this silent forest.

I turned back, letting everything wash over me. My hooves sunk into the wet ground along the riverbank, making the walk difficult. The clang of my armour echoed through the quiet woods.

Finally, I reached the spot where we had separated, and I waited. Delsaran returned a few minutes later. He smiled, but I could tell by his face that he was not celebrating victory. And I was sure he could tell by my face that I had not found anything either.

When he reached me, he put his meaty hand on my shoulder. I had grown taller than him, but I still felt his reassurance.

"I'm sorry, Chase," he said, his voice soft and smooth. "But I know we're getting closer. We've found more old gouges in the trees, each scored at a different time. We'll find them."

He meant well, and I appreciated that. "Thank you," I said.

Delsaran turned to walk deeper into the forest, and my question came pouring out. "How do you love everything?" Delsaran's eyes widened. "I make myself accept things. I deaden myself to the cruelties of the world. I've done it for as long as I can remember, and I know it's unhealthy, but any time I stop, I just hate everything."

Delsaran hugged me. I wished my head still fit into his chest.

He pulled back and spoke. "People think that love is selfless, Chase.

"Bullshit." He laughed. Then he saw the earnestness in my face and considered his words. "Or, incomplete. Love is as selfish as it is selfless."

Delsaran studied the water flowing over the jagged rocks. "Love is like water. It swells from a thousand little streams—a melting glacier, an underground spring, fall rain. Together, they form a mighty river that brings life to the world around it and carves canyons through the hardest rock."

Delsaran opened his arms. "But a river gives exactly as much as it takes. Some try to push their water to dry, loveless lands. But without streams to feed it, that once-mighty river dries to a brook, then a trickle, and ends as a stagnant puddle. Others try to damn their river and hoard a reservoir of love. But still water turns foul and loses its power to erode the hard and strong."

Delsaran took my hands in his. "To love freely is to know what feeds you and hold tight to it, no matter how strange to yourself or others. Make it yours. Then take all your love and pour it back into the world. As it flows, you will find more streams to feed you and make you stronger." Delsaran looked at the world around him. His face was radiant.

"Loving openly, we find more love."

I pondered Delsaran's words. What did feeding myself even mean?

I tried to open myself to the sun, as Delsaran said in his mantra, and let it fill me. I could see the red light shine through my eyelids.

But I just felt mildly warm.

I tried to listen to the sounds of the forest around me, but there were none. All was silent but for the rush of the water against the rocks.

That was odd.

"Have you heard any animals since we crossed the river?"

Delsaran cocked his head. "Not that I can think of," he said. "No, there's been nothing. I hadn't noticed that." He put his hand on my shoulder. "Good job, Chase."

I smiled, wide and proud.

Delsaran leaned down and touched the ground. His fingertips glowed, but it was a duller white than before.

"There's almost no energy to channel here," he said. "It's like something stripped the life out of the land. The plants didn't die, but they're not growing well. And there's no wildlife around here." He looked up at me. "We might have found it."

"There were a lot of gouges in the trees before the river, but after, there were none," I said.

Delsaran frowned. "That might mean there were no animals left to attack." His voice was slow and heavy. "Something happened here." He looked around. "But I don't see any evidence of it."

Delsaran put his hand down to the ground again. It glowed a dull, faint grey as he turned it in a big circle. "It's stronger that way," he said, pointing into the forest. "I feel less energy, at least."

Then he looked at me. "Better check your weapons and armour," he said. "We might need them soon."

I checked my blade and made sure it was solidly attached to the haft. My shield straps were secure. And my breastplate didn't budge as I moved.

I looked over at Delsaran just as he finished checking his sword for any nicks or cracks. Satisfied, he looked at me. "Ready to be a hero, Chase?" he asked.

"You know it," I said. I hiked my axe over my shoulder, then we walked deeper into the woods.

But with every step, the pit of fear in my belly grew bigger. How would we stop this? Was I ready to face whatever we would find with only Delsaran at my side?

Our route here had been circuitous, following gouges and guesses; we could make it back to Greenchapel in a couple days. If this were the place, we could go back and bring a group, ready to take on whatever we find.

Delsaran strode forward, confident and determined. His eyes looked deep within the trees for whatever they could find.

I tried to imitate him, watching the shadows that covered the ground. I held my axe ready in case our eyes missed something that would spring upon us.

Finally, we came upon some sort of circular clearing. It stretched out into the distance; it would take at least five minutes to walk from one end to the other.

Though *clearing* was perhaps the wrong word for it. A better one might be *tree graveyard*. Trunks littered the ground, collapsed one on top of the other. Toward the edge of the clearing, one or two had a small splat of moss, but the rest of the toppled trees looked preserved, as though they had dried, undecomposed. Even the grass had died. The still forest wind had uprooted it, leaving its yellow-brown blades and dark roots scattered along the ground.

Delsaran put his palm against my chest and stopped me. "This was powerful magic. I have never seen its like." He studied the clearing closely. "Death should always feed new life. But here, there is nothing.

"This is not a place of death; it is a place of annihilation."

He touched the ground with his hand as he continued scanning the clearing. "But it looks like whatever caused this is gone. I'd say this happened a few years ago—right before Greenchapel was first attacked by the nightbringers. But be careful; whatever caused this is too powerful for my magic to stop. If we set it off, well . . ."

Delsaran looked at me. His eyes were soft and full of love.

I cursed myself for my fear, for wanting to go back and bring others in my place. That was a Jon answer, I knew. Here, we do what needs doing.

Delsaran stepped forward, and I followed. I closed my eyes as I walked into the clearing. I imagined the magic would feel like a waterfall washing over me. Instead, I simply walked through the silence of this barren space.

Delsaran scrutinized every patch of ground as he picked his way across the clearing. He looked ready to pull back at the slightest warning.

My hand clenched the handle of my axe as I scanned the ground with him. I readied myself to strike any foe or leap back from any trap. My ears strained to take in the slightest sound that presaged danger.

But the only sounds were the cracking of dry branches beneath our feet and hooves.

Finally, we reached the centre of the clearing. There was a hole in the ground, about the size of a door. Stairs disappeared into the darkness.

Delsaran stopped and touched the ground again. "I don't feel any magic trying to harm us," he said. "I feel"—he closed his eyes, focussing on the ground—"nothing."

I knew Delsaran well enough to hear the slight edge to his voice. My muscles tensed, and my mind screamed at me to run away. If the person who created this wanted to avoid being found, why would they allow everything around them to die? If they didn't care about being found, why did it take us so long to find it?

Delsaran checked his pack and weapons, making sure they were strapped tight. "Are you ready, Chase?"

I nodded automatically.

Delsaran took a last look at the trees on the horizon. Then he closed his eyes and spread his arms, his head tilted back to feel the sun on his face.

He repeated his mantra one last time. I imitated his pose and said it with him, though the words felt hollow to me. His muscles relaxed, but did not rest; cat-like, they looked ready to pounce. When he finished, his body had uncharacteristic grace, each muscle moving with precision.

Then he smiled at me, and I could see the genuine happiness on his face. He reached up to rub my head.

"I love you, Chase," he said.

"And I love you, Delsaran."

He hugged me, then. His arms went around my lower back and pulled me against him, my muzzle resting against his ear. My arms wrapped around his shoulders, and, for the first time, I pulled him against me. I held him against my chest, taking every bit of love he had and giving all of mine in return.

Then, without a word, he broke the hug, turned, and descended the stairs.

He became darker and darker with each step. In seconds, his form was reduced to the faintest of silhouettes, and I knew that, if I waited a moment longer, he would disappear completely.

I followed him into the dark.

DEPTHS

We climbed down the stairs, and the sunlight faded. But as my eyes adjusted, I realised I could see well. Small crystals, embedded in the walls, gave off light as we approached them, and I could study the stairwell in detail.

It was roughly chiseled from the bedrock, with peaks and divots everywhere. Yet the surface was smooth and shiny, as though it had been polished. The ceiling was unsupported by any bolts or planks, and I could spy no ventilation shafts. Yet the stairs were free of the smallest rocks, and the air smelled fresh and clear. This had been carved by magic.

Delsaran touched one of the little light crystals, his face pensive. "They're no ward or alarm," he said. "Just illumination. I hope that whoever built this thought its remoteness would shield it from intrusion." He peered down into the darkness. "Seems safe enough for now."

I nodded, my hands tight on my axe. Delsaran's body was relaxed, and his sword was sheathed, but his hand never strayed too far from his sword's hilt.

The stairs soon opened into what looked like the inside of a house. We stood in some sort of hallway; on either side, arches of rock opened into rooms.

In the closest room, an oven had been carved into the far wall, and a fire pit beneath it. On the right side of the room, a long counter ran from one wall to the other. It was hewn from the same rock as the walls, but it reflected the crystals like a mirror. On the left side of the room, crates of food were stacked, perhaps enough to feed a person for a year.

Delsaran walked into the room, and I followed. I brushed my fingers against the counter, and they glided across its smooth surface.

I stopped. Something about this kitchen triggered a memory of Jon's speeches about mining—the fire pit. I crept closer to the pit and realised the top had spalled, leaving a small pile of rock flakes at the bottom, but there was no ash from whatever fueled the fire.

"That oven has been heated by magic," I told Delsaran.

Delsaran looked at the stone flakes. "Good eye, Chase," he said. He crouched down by the pantry. "And these turnips have withered from age yet are free of mold." Delsaran stood. "I suspect this place has been abandoned—for one reason or another."

I looked around to find more clues, but saw only knives, rolling pins, spoons, and tongs arrayed on the counter for use.

"I don't think we'll find anything else here," Delsaran said softly. "Let's keep exploring,"

But the other rooms provided little else in the way of information. There was a bedroom, which, like everything else, was sparsely decorated. It did, however, have a real bed that would match Jon's for quality—one of the few things here not made from the bedrock. This mage knew the value of a good night's sleep.

Next was a library, bookshelves carved into the walls and filled with books on various magical subjects. The only furniture was a single armchair with a long back and luscious upholstery. We looked through the titles of the books, but aside from an unusual number of books on the transmutation of raw magic, there was little that caught our eyes.

The last room was round; a bench, covered by goatskin, protruded from the wall. The skin was roughly cut, so it was most likely local. In the centre of the room sat a table with runes carved into it. I suspected it was magic but could make nothing of the runes.

Delsaran put his hand against it. "It's some kind of . . ." he began. "I'm not sure, but I think I might be able to see what the mage did with it last." Delsaran looked at me, his eyes probing. "But not knowing what this does, that could be dangerous."

I looked back at him with my practiced listening face.

"Then again," he said, "we haven't discovered much else."

His hand glowed, then the wall turned blue near the top and green near the bottom. The colours became shapes, then resolved into grass and sky. Along the grass, a brown jousting fence came into focus. On the left, a knight in green sat upon a black horse; on the right, a knight in red sat upon a white horse.

A horn blew behind me, and I turned to see stands and heralds, all watching the knights prepare. Then the knights lowered their lances and dropped their visors. The horn blew again, and the knights charged. As their horses' hooves pounded the dirt, they grew larger and larger until they took up the whole wall. Then they leapt through the wall and crashed into each other above me.

The crack of lance against shield filled the room, and the red knight toppled from his horse. He hit the ground at my feet with a thud, then everything disappeared, and the room was black.

It took a moment for my eyes to readjust to the dull glow of the crystals.

Delsaran looked at the table with wonder. "This is a feat of magic, not for power or prestige, but to manage being out here, alone."

He grazed his fingertips along the table. "Everything we've seen here, other than the bed, chair, and books, this wizard has built themself. I admire their self-reliance. But this still gives us no clue about what happened here."

I swallowed. The further we got, the more it seemed we learned nothing. We were wandering in blind when we should be bringing an army. I had to say something.

"Jon always told me that we were stronger and freer as a society," I managed. "Should we get an army?"

"Oh, Chase," Delsaran said. "That is never the solution. Let me explain.

"Some people hate Jon because he's selfish." Delsaran waggled his fingers, saying "Oooooo" like a ghost. Then he laughed.

"Yes, he is selfish. We all are. We take care of ourselves and our loved ones."

Delsaran sighed. "Jon harnesses that selfishness to create wealth. And it works! But when you create a society based on competition . . ."

Delsaran shook his head. "Imagine we're all fishing from a lake. Each of us fishes enough to feed our families and earn a small living, and the fish population remains stable. Then one person invents a new fishing net that catches more. They become rich. The fish population declines, and suddenly no one else can feed their family. Faced with starvation, everyone adopts the new net and empties the lake of fish. Everything and everyone are ruined."

Delsaran held up his arms helplessly. "What can stop this race to the bottom? In a massive society with their armies, you must give someone else power—priests, kings, generals—who enforce unwieldy laws that imprison us in their narrow, inflexible vision.

"Yes, Greenchapel is poor on its own." Delsaran took my hands in his. "But what really matters is protected."

He hugged me, and I felt so full of love. I took his words and warmth into my heart; as battered as I had been by life, my heart felt full.

"Ready, Chase?" Delsaran asked.

I nodded, and we walked down the stairs. My hands gripped the haft of my axe. In the stories Bri told, traps, mazes, and monsters always waited deeper.

But the stairwell merely opened into a single room, large and well-lit from the crystals implanted in the walls. Runes ran down those walls and into the floor, leading to a small plinth in the middle of the room, upon which lay a black crystal.

And next to that lay a body.

Its skin was a dark grey-brown and drawn over the bones of its hands and face. The body looked unnaturally thin, as though it had no muscle or fat, or even lungs and stomach. Its clothes seemed made for a bigger man, spread out over the floor around it.

Delsaran approached the body and kneeled beside it. He ran a finger under the clothes, lifting them and looking beneath. I felt my stomach churn, and I looked away.

"This body dried long ago, like everything else here," Delsaran finally said. I could hear him moving, but I didn't look. "But there was nothing to decompose it. It just lay here as the moisture evaporated."

I could hear Delsaran walk toward me. He put his hand on my shoulder and squeezed. I leaned against his touch.

"I know it's hard. But it's worse than you know." I turned and saw the sadness in his eyes. "Andarta was right, and she's going to lord this over me for months." Delsaran sighed dramatically. Despite the timing of the joke, I smiled.

"That mage unleashed some magic he couldn't control and died with everything else. I don't know what he was trying to do. But I suspect that, if we destroy the crystal, we—" Delsaran pushed me away from him.

I fell back, the world a blur, and I heard Delsaran's palm smack against the handle of his sword. The world went white as his blade rang free of its scabbard.

By the time my eyes adjusted, the nightbringer was already dust. But two more were rushing toward us, and three black and red arms reached out of the crystal in the centre of the room.

Without the archers to slow them, the creatures sped across the room on long strides of their spindly legs.

But Delsaran and I had been training for them.

Delsaran sprinted forward to meet the nightbringers. They swung their arms at his pale flesh, leaving red streaks in my vision. But Delsaran had the range advantage. He sliced off the arm of the closest one, then ducked under the arms of the second.

The nightbringer swung its arms again, a red and black blur aimed at his head, but Delsaran spun and took it out at the knee. It keeled over, its arms flailing through the air, and landed in front of Delsaran as it turned to dust.

Delsaran leapt over it, ready to sprint forward again.

But the crystal spewed out more nightbringers. Three met him as he landed, attacking at once.

Delsaran dodged to the right. Two of the creatures groped at the space he had been a moment before, but he didn't get enough distance from the third. It swung its arm at his face; Delsaran pitched back, and the arm passed just over him before he righted himself and cut the nightbringer in two.

The other two nightbringers were on him now, and more emerged from the crystal every second, their arms digging into the ground to pull them out.

I ran.

I reached Delsaran's side as he dusted the two nightbringers and stepped back to avoid the arms of five more. My skin tingled from the heat radiating off them, but I knew how to deal with them.

The nightbringer on my left was closer, so I waited until it was just in range, then swung. My axe cleaved through its torso; it disintegrated in a second, its outstretched arms falling at my feet before disappearing. I swung my axe back across my body to slice through the second and scatter its dust.

A blow hit my shield, and I staggered back. Two more nightbringers were already on top of me, and only Delsaran's drilling about keeping my shield up had saved me. I took a step back to try to get some distance, but they were faster, their hands reaching around my shield and stretching for my face.

Then Delsaran charged into them. His speed carried a single swing of his glowing sword through them both.

"If I can reach the crystal, we can stop this!" he shouted as he turned to face the onslaught of nightbringers. They came out of the crystal so fast I could barely see it past their void-like bodies.

Delsaran's blade was a blur as he fended off the arms reaching toward him, but not even he could keep his ground. Each time he stepped back, three nightbringers would turn to dust, but four more took their place. They all focused on him.

That left me with an opening. I dashed forward, axe swinging.

I cut through the first two easily, their arms never even turning toward me. I swung back across my body, taking out two more. Delsaran held his ground, slicing through the remaining nightbringers as fast as they arrived.

Then the nightbringers coming out of the crystal swarmed me.

I had just enough time to raise my shield before the screech of their pointy hands against steel filled the room. I slammed my shoulder into my shield, trying to knock them back. A couple reeled, stumbling, but the arms of the rightmost nightbringer barely moved.

But that one was closest to my axe.

I swung as hard as I could. My axe cleaved through the nightbringer's torso—and the one beside it. But my swing slid only partway into the torso of the third one before my axe stopped. Then the nightbringers I had knocked back with my shield recovered and came for me again.

I leapt back, pulling my axe free and watching the nightbringer re-form. Slowed by my wound, the other nightbringers swept around it, pressing up against my shield and reaching for my flesh.

I choked up on my axe, and hacked through arms where I could, but not fast enough. Black and red arms grazed my armour. I had to keep retreating.

Delsaran stood his ground, still trying to drive forward. His glowing sword sliced through the nightbringers with ease, but without me beside him, his flank was exposed. Even his blur of a sword couldn't go from side to side fast enough to catch every arm. The steel of his armour softened beneath the heat of their blows.

"We're not going to be able to push through them!" I shouted to Delsaran. It had taken the entire town of Greenchapel to battle a huge mass before.

"We will!" Delsaran shouted back. "I've just got to get to that crystal!"

I tried to push myself harder, but my body didn't respond. My armour felt heavy on my shoulders and my arms ached.

At this rate, we had no chance. Delsaran needed me to hold his flank if he was going to get to the crystal, and I retreated further from him with each step.

We just do what needs doing.

I gritted my teeth and dropped my shield.

Wielding my axe with both hands, my swing sailed through one, then two, then three, then four nightbringers, clearing the space in front of me. I took a step forward and swung again. My axe went harder and wider, cleaving through them as fast as they could charge.

I swung again. One escaped my axe, and attacked me from the side, its arms speeding towards me. I inched forward and swung again, but not before I felt the tip of its limb hit my arm; the heat burned through layers of wool, fur, and skin before I cut it in half.

I kept going. I took another step and put my hips into my swing, my whole body turning with my axe. I exposed my back with each swing, but it was the only chance I had. I had to trust my strength and speed to carry me through.

I stepped forward. My axe head careened through the nightbringers coming toward me. They died so fast all I saw was their dust. If I could just protect Delsaran's flank, we'd make it to the crystal. As fast and hard as I could, I swung my axe again.

But one of the nightbringers was faster. It struck the back of my hand. I felt my flesh char, and every part of my arm burned.

I twisted back as fast as I could to cut through the creature, but the pain was too much; my axe slipped out of my hands and clattered to the ground.

"Delsaran!" I screamed. I stumbled back as the nightbringers swarmed me.

Delsaran turned as my arms flailed, and he ran toward me, his sword incandescent.

But the nightbringers were still closer. My hooves skittered along the ground as I backpedalled. Then I stepped on my shield, and it flew out from under me.

I tumbled over, landing on my back. I gasped for air as the nightbringers surrounded me.

Their hands burned me. The metal of my armour seared my skin. I tried to crawl away, but my limbs didn't respond.

Then Delsaran's glowing white blade sliced through them. They turned to dust as he grabbed my breastplate and hauled me to my hooves. But as I stood, he hissed, and his face contorted. Two nightbringers' hands dug into his back.

His sword flickered for a moment, and then shone like the sun, turning the whole room white. Faster than I had ever seen anyone move, he spun and cut through the creatures behind him.

"Up the stairs!" he shouted, his voice horse.

I ran, my hooves slapping hard on the rock. I heard Delsaran a step behind me, his boots only slightly quieter on the stairs.

We reached the top of the stairs and kept running. My chest and legs burned, and my arm hung limply by my side. I focused on the stairs leading outside. I just had to reach them. My legs had to hold out just a little longer.

Then I was yanked sideways through the air. For a moment, I had no idea what was happening. Then I looked up into Delsaran's ruddy face, his finger on his lips, which pulsed with each of his heavy breaths.

He pulled me down and underneath a smooth counter and clutched me tight to his chest. We were in the kitchen.

I couldn't understand what was going on. We were helpless here. Even if we got out from under the counter in time, we would never be able to escape the kitchen.

I looked toward the archway. I couldn't see through it. All I could do was wait for the nightbringers to pour in.

But as the seconds passed, they didn't come. Our heaving breaths slowed, and, bit by bit, our bodies relaxed.

The exhaustion hit me at once. My limbs felt like lead. I could only rest my head on Delsaran's chest. My vision started to go dark.

I listened to Delsaran's slow, strong heart, and felt safe.

SORROW

"Chase," Delsaran whispered as he shook me awake. His fingers gripped my shoulders, and his breath was dry against my face. I stifled a cry.

Every part of me ached. My neck, my legs, my arms, my chest. My muscles cramped, and my flesh burned. I looked down at my body. Over the sharpest pain, my armour was warped and bulbous.

"They're gone now," Delsaran said.

I nodded—speaking still felt too dangerous. I tried to stretch out the knots in my body and straighten my arms and legs—only to pull them back in as the muscles seized.

I breathed and, eventually, the pain passed. I crawled off Delsaran, favouring my left arm. I tried to relax, but I kept glancing toward the archway. I had to know if they were gone. I inched over to the arch. Slowly, the hallway came into view.

It was empty.

The nightbringers would have gone in a straight line until they found other prey. We were safe.

If we had gone up like I had planned, they would have seen us in the clearing, and we would have had to keep running. Weighed down by armour and wounded from battle, I don't think we would have made it.

Delsaran had saved my life.

I stood, stretching out my back as I did so. Delsaran followed me to his feet, giving me a chance to look at him. Small blisters covered his arms, the skin flaky between them. The polish on his breastplate was broken by streaks of dull grey, but it looked like the injuries were skin-deep.

Until he turned and I saw his back. The nightbringers who attacked him while he was lifting me to my feet had melted through his armour and charred his skin black.

"Krek," I whispered. "Are you all right?"

"I'm alive, and you're alive," he said. "What else is there to desire?" Then he looked at my axe arm; it hung by my side. "Though I should check that out," he said.

He leaned in close to look at my hand; his beard tickled my fur. "A lot of your fur was burnt off, and the skin here is broken," he said. "But no serious damage was done."

He tore a piece of cloth from his shirt and wrapped it around my hand, then touched my hand with his own. It glowed for a moment, and my hand felt warm and cool at the same time.

"Bandage it and keep it clean, and your arm will be back to normal soon," he said.

I nodded. "How about your back?"

He grimaced, then laughed. "That will take a bit longer to heal. But it will." He put his hand on my shoulder. "Come, Chase," he said, "let's go back down before another horde spawns."

He picked up his sword and led the way downstairs. As he climbed down, he kept his back rigid.

When we reached the bottom of the stairs, Delsaran strode right to the crystal, his step more relaxed on even ground. But I kept my back against the wall. I knew how the nightbringers hunted, but I felt that some nightbringers might have lingered here, ready to attack again. Finding none, I crept over to my axe and shield, glancing behind me just in case.

Delsaran, his hands glowing, touched the crystal. "It absorbed a lot of life energy when it was created but seems to run on its own power now. Its energy is building, but a long way from full." He focused on the crystal. "I'd guess about two days before another group comes forth. But I can't figure out more than that."

I checked the stairwell to make sure no nightbringers had followed us down as I walked over to Delsaran. "What can we do about it?" I asked.

Delsaran gestured to the floor and walls. "I don't recognise these runes. I don't know the magic behind this." Delsaran breathed heavily. "I'm back at plan A: hit it with my sword."

"Could we get a mage? Or learn about it in the library?" I asked.

"There are no mages that could understand this in Greenchapel. And we could spend a year in that library before we even started to understand this," Delsaran responded. "Neither of us have the background in magical theory."

I was good with books. Jon had always told me so.

But Delsaran had sounded certain. And this is what we did here: what needs doing. I had felt the truth of that. The fire had burned in my belly.

Delsaran unsheathed his sword and held it in front of his face with both hands. "Hacky-slash it is," he said, smiling.

He closed his eyes and breathed. His sword began to glow.

"I open myself to your light,
    And you fill me.
I open my body to your warm caress,
    And you melt idle lethargy with joy and love.
I open my mind to your radiant serenity,
    And you bore through petty distractions with devotion.
I open my soul to your inferno,
    And you incinerate the stupor of self-doubt with passion.

"With the ecstasy of joy and love,
    I will nurture my fire.
With the clarity of devotion,
    I will carry my flame into the darkness.
With the resolve of passion,
    I will burn and bring light to the world."

With each word, his sword shone brighter, pulsing with the movements of his chest until there was nothing but its white light and the black crystal beneath it. I stared into the light; despite its radiance, it didn't hurt my eyes at all.

I had seen his magic before, but this was the first time I felt it—the sheer brilliance of his magic, filling everything that was, everything that ever would be. I felt the full force of his love manifest. It was divine and feral, selfish and selfless, furious and serene.

It was life itself.

Then he swung.

A deafening crack of sound and magic lifted me off my hooves and slammed my back against the wall. The world went dark as the breath was knocked out of me, and I collapsed to the floor.

My eyes struggled to pierce the darkness. Had I been blinded by the impact? Or had Delsaran's blade gone out?

Slowly, shapes began to take form. Delsaran staggered around the crystal. He still held his sword, but it was just the grey of steel.

The middle of the crystal had been cracked, deep and wide, almost cutting it in two; smaller cracks wormed through the rest of the crystal. But even I could feel it hum with power.

Delsaran prepared to strike again. He lifted his sword, then, still a bit off-balance, put his empty hand on the crystal to steady himself.

His hand withered and turned grey.

Delsaran yanked his hand back and looked at me, his eyes and mouth wide. "Chase, get out of here!" he screamed. Then his sword glowed, but nowhere near as bright as before. He brought the sword down hard, and the crack deepened, but the crystal did not break.

Black limbs emerged from the crystal, each one jagged like a lightning bolt. Delsaran hacked at them, slicing through as many as he could with each swipe. They fell to the floor and turned to dust—but were replaced by more.

And Delsaran was beginning to slow.

Each limb became longer before Delsaran could slash through it. Craggy, misshapen torsos followed the limbs. Then blocky, lopsided heads. Finally, whole nightbringers emerged, misshapen monstrosities of chaotic, broken magic.

Delsaran's grey hand hung limply by his side, and his sword's light flickered.

"Chase, run!" he screamed.

For a moment, I froze. *Rewards from obedience,* I heard. But this was Delsaran.

I ran—toward Delsaran, my axe held high.

Delsaran's eyes glistened with love and sadness. He pointed his sword at me, and, for a moment, it glowed bright again. Then a gust of wind lifted me and carried me up the stairs.

"No!" I screamed. "No!"

I struggled against the wind, but it was no use.

Through tears, I could see the light from his sword flicker once, then twice, and then a third time.

Then go out.

The wind dissipated, and, slowly, I fell to the ground and landed with a soft thud.

I sprang to my feet and charged down the stairs.

A black and red mass of gnarled limbs and heat blocked my path at the bottom of the stairs.

I hacked through it with all my might. I swung and swung again. Flecks of magic dust filled the stairwell, and the flesh of my legs sizzled as the twisted mass touched me.

I only thought of Delsaran.

These malformed nightbringers moved slowly, their stunted, bent limbs inching over the ground. But they oozed forward relentlessly. My swings were as useless as trying to empty an ocean with a bucket. It didn't matter. I would keep going until I had drained it dry.

Then I saw it—too late. One nightbringer had crawled within the arc of my swing, and its crooked limb reached for the shaft of my axe as I swung down. Its arm burned right through the shaft, and my axe head clattered to the ground. I was left with nothing but a stick.

I swung it anyway, trying to bash them away, but the stick burned in seconds and scorched the flesh of my hand.

I held my shield in front of me and drove my shoulder into it, desperate to bash through. But the nightbringers didn't budge. They filled the stairwell from top to bottom and drove me up them even as their touch burned my legs. And my shield was quickly becoming too hot to hold.

What little remained of the world became saturated with tears.

I dropped my shield and ran.

DESCENT

I thought I would never stop running.

NADIR

My lungs struggled to inhale the viscous, stagnant cloud of air around me as I scarcely dodged the vague shadows of tree trunks. Their branches dug into my face and arms as I passed them. My hooves sunk into the soft ground as it tried to swallow me.

One thick branch caught my armour and lifted me off my feet. Then I fell, hard, on my numb ass.

I tore at the armour. My fingers dug into the straps and tried to pull them off, but the breastplate stuck on my muzzle. I yanked at it over and over, my head swinging wildly with each tug. Finally, the branch snapped, and I stumbled free.

I could feel the smooth steel against my fingers, and I remembered Delsaran's smiling face as he gave it to me.

I ran.

My hooves barely lifted off the ground. The tips of them dragged through the dirt.

I had run through these shadows before, when Rorvin lay bleeding on the ground. Bri stood over him, yelling at me to fetch his mother.

Even in my haze, I knew I had no Avinna to run to this time. I just had to keep running. Even as I stumbled over every bump and pit. Even as my ankles ached from rolling over rock and root.

But the years spent trekking through this forest had still left me with limits. I tried to lift my leg for another step, but it didn't respond. I pitched forward; my arm reached out and caught a tree next to me.

I sank down to the ground as my chest heaved.

I had hoped that, if I couldn't run any more, I would fall and let the void overcome me.

Instead, I felt everything.

My head pounded. My legs ached. Delsaran's red beard rubbed against my head as he held me. Delsaran's eyes stared into mine, soft with love.

I forced myself to stand. I gripped the tree and pulled myself to my knees. Then I lifted one foot, and, finally, I hauled myself to my hooves. I turned and tried to run again.

My hooves caught in the dirt, and I was forced to grab the tree again. I walked.

I walked as the sun set. I walked as the moon rose. I walked as the stars glowed through the wet darkness. I walked as my eyes closed from exhaustion, and I stumbled into rocks and trees.

I walked until there was nothing but the void left. Nothingness from every nerve, even as my legs collapsed.

I fell, and my consciousness became part of the void.

Even closed, my eyes burned from the red glare of the sun. The ground was hard and cold against my aching shoulder. Every muscle in my body was cramped and knotted.

I lay unmoving, hoping the void would overtake me again.

I knew I would feel better if I stretched, if I moved, if I ate, if I drank. I had always taken care of my body, and that had given me the strength to get through anything. Just endure the pain, I had told myself, and things would get better—eventually.

Now I just wanted to lie until leaves covered me and I decomposed into soil. I would become part of a tree, reaching for the same sun my mother spoke of.

But my thirst grew until all my suffering was mere background noise to my aching throat. I sat up, my stiff body protesting every movement. I grabbed my water pouch and drank. I gulped the water down as fast as I could. Soon—far too soon—the pouch was as dry as my throat.

My stomach rumbled. I pulled out a Tubelicious, and bit into it. It tasted as it always did, flaky and savoury. It filled me up quickly, but my throat still felt dry. I would need to get more water. Thankfully, that was something Delsaran had taught me how to do.

Like most of my memories of Delsaran, it began with his smile. *Life depends on water,* he said. *Remember that, and you'll always find it.* He reached down to the grass, still wet with the morning dew, and gently lifted a droplet off a stalk. *Walk through this with cloths on your legs, and you can wring them out to meet your morning thirst.*

Then he pointed to the tree above us, where some apples hung. *Fruits and many vegetables will have enough water to keep you going until you find a stream.* Finally, he pointed down to a break in the grass, where hoofprints lay. *And the animals who live here know where to find water. Follow a trail downhill, and you'll find water soon enough.*

Delsaran, saving my life once again.

I dug my fingers into my leg and let it hurt.

The dew had cleared while I lay upon the ground, but the rest of his advice would hold. I found an animal trail and followed it down. I pulled what fruit I could from trees and bushes—blueberries, black-berries, and some crab-apples.

Finally, I could hear the dull roar of rapids through the trees. I couldn't pinpoint its direction, but I kept following the trail. Soon, I came upon a river, the water white as it rushed over rocks and clear where the stream flattened.

I kneeled in the wet grass beside the stream, filled my pouch, and drank. I felt my mind clear, as though the water washed away the gunk clogging it.

I preferred my mind clogged.

I wanted to cry, to scream, to tear my brain from my skull. But I couldn't even breathe. I felt myself drowning in air, like a fish left on the dock.

Slowly, the world turned black as I struggled to cry. I began to topple into the stream, and, for a moment, I just let it happen. The stream would carry me until I fed a mighty river.

Then my muzzle hit the water. I choked as it flowed down my throat and filled by lungs. By instinct, I pushed myself out of the water, the rocks digging into my hands.

I coughed so hard I thought my chest would explode.

Eventually, my coughs subsided, and my throat opened enough to take a gasping breath.

I rolled onto my back. The water covered my ears but left my muzzle free. I panted, loud and hoarse. Tears streamed down my face.

I had been lonely for so much of my life. But I had always been in the shadow of others, of Bri, Jon, and Delsaran. I lived in their homes and called them my own. I followed their wisdom and believed it my own.

I had been taken from one home by laws that decreed I was not a person, and from the other by monsters I didn't understand.

I had been Jon's slave. I had been Bri's friend. I had been Delsaran's son.

Now I was just a minotaur in a forest.

Alone.

ALONE

The water flowed past my head, pulling my fur along with it. The sun hung in the sky above me, its rays carrying a flat, muted heat.

"It's the same sun," I said, then coughed out a hollow laugh.

I had spent so many days looking up at that sun, trying to find the inspiration my mom and Delsaran had taken from it. And now, though it shone high in the sky, it left me cold.

My mother had said our gods would protect me here; whenever I missed home, I could look up and be connected to it. But I no longer felt like I had a home to be connected to.

Delsaran had told me to just live in the moment, and relish in its warmth and life. And he stuck to that, even as it killed him.

I cried. Angry, sad, bitter, resentful, lonely tears.

As the sun set, my tears dried. I felt more exhausted than I had on any of those days I had hiked thirty miles after sleeping on grass for months.

I was too tired to feel angry anymore. Too tired to even feel sad. I had been emptied out.

I lay there as the sky turned black.

I awoke shivering.

The sky was still black above me. Not even a halo of light lit the horizon. But I needed to do something about the cold.

I crawled out of the stream and shivered. My fur was soaked through, and my wool shirt hung heavy on my shoulders. Both took the heat from my body and dripped it on the ground.

I took off my shirt and wrung it out, then shook off as much water as I could from my fur. I checked my armour and scrubbed the worst of the rust off. I considered putting my shirt in my pack, but that would just soak everything else.

Thankfully, the wind was gentle. If the wind were strong, I would have to strip naked and climb beneath a bed of dry leaves to keep out the chill.

Tonight, walking would warm me enough. I looked for Qhyton's star, shining bright in the night. If I kept it on my left, I would walk into Orachim. Eventually, I'd find a road or farm that would lead me back to a city. From there, I'd be able to find Greenchapel again.

Was there anything I wanted to go back to Greenchapel for?

I wasn't sure.

But it was a plan. And any plan seemed good enough right now. So, I walked through the night. Slowly, my clothes dried, then my fur. I warmed—slightly.

The horizon turned a dark blue, and I knew dawn would break soon. But I had no energy to face the sunrise.

I gathered a few leaves to blunt the hardness of the ground, then lay down to sleep.

The sun blazed bright into my eyes. It had risen well above the trees, so I must have slept through most of the morning.

I was stiff, but, thankfully, warm. I tried to stretch out, but my back and legs cramped, and I curled into a ball. When the spasms passed, I tried again, slowly. Though my muscles protested, and I had to be careful of my wounds, I was able to move.

I stood and felt the sun on my body. I tried to bask in it and forget what happened, and I almost succeeded, but then my chest seized, and the pain came roaring back.

I sighed. It was time to go back to what I knew: ignore the pain and take care of my body, hoping one day things would get better.

The first order of business was water and food. I wrapped my shirt around my legs and gathered what remained of the dew while I wandered around, finding some berries and nuts.

Then I started walking. I kept the sun on my left as I walked past forest and meadow, over hill and valley, and through brook and stream. I took a drink from any river that flowed fast and clear enough and rested when the heat of the sun became oppressive. Then I kept walking.

I kept my eyes open for food as I walked but mostly ate Tubelicious. I didn't want to stray from my path to forage.

I watched the sky turn red, purple, then black. I built another bed of leaves beneath a tree and lay down.

I thought of Greenchapel. I told myself they needed to know what happened. They needed to protect themselves.

But as I slept, I dreamt only of Delsaran's smile, and the twang of Bri's bow.

That morning, the rain came down hard.

I had mostly managed to stay dry; the water had sloughed off the leaves of the tree above me. But some water trickled down, wetting my woolens and the leaves beneath me.

I considered staying beneath the tree all day, and just letting the rain pass. But the more I lay there, the more my thoughts circled upon themselves, and my mood grew worse.

So, I stripped off my clothes and put them in my pack with my armour. Naked, I walked through the rain, letting it run down my fur and skin. It was cold and miserable, but focusing on that kept my mind off thoughts that hurt more.

The clouds hid the sun, so I had to guess which way was forward. But, from time to time, a slight break in the dark sky would be outlined in brilliant white, and I could readjust, and continue.

That night, though I was exhausted, I lay awake for what felt like hours as the rain poured down. I wondered how Bri was living his life. Was he still with Jon? Or had he started his own adventures as the archer he had always dreamed of becoming?

Was he happy?

The rain had stopped by the time I awoke, but clouds still scattered the sunlight. Everything had a flat, lifeless look, its shadows diffused.

The rain had pooled on leaves, so I could drink while leaving my pouch full. I found a few fruits and nuts and supplemented them with a piece of Tubelicious.

Then I walked.

The sun lifted itself into the sky above me, and I rested in the shade. Then, as the sun passed its zenith, I continued.

When the sun rested just above my shoulder, streaking the clouds in front of me yellow, I came upon a path. It was not a big path—no more than some wagon tracks in the grass, and a trail of earth where the horses walked. Water pooled in fresh hoofprints, so I knew the path was still in use.

I looked for any sign of which way to go, but I saw nothing but trees and grass. I had to simply pick a direction and walk.

I dressed, then turned right and walked along the trail. My hooves sunk into the wet ground, but my steps felt lighter than they had since . . . that place.

The sky in front of me turned orange, red, then dark grey. I kept walking. Finally, as the stars twinkled above, I saw the outline of a small castle against the black sky. Beneath it, I could see small pinpricks of light from the houses of the town. I had made it.

Because of Delsaran.

My hooves slipped on the wet ground as I walked toward the castle. But as the night deepened, the path became paved, and farmers' fields stretched out perpendicular to the road, their crops almost as tall as me. In far-off windows, candlelight flickered.

My legs and mind protested, but I was almost there. I walked on as the castle grew bigger, and candles were lit and blown out.

Finally, the fields gave way to markets and stores. My eyes strained to make out their names in the darkness: baker, smithy, witch, couper, abecedarian. Then The Rusty Nail Inn. Its sign had a pockmarked nail above a bed. I walked inside.

Tables covered the ground floor. They were sparsely populated now, though a few flagons rested on empty tables, yet to be taken away.

Most of the people there looked like farmers, thick and sun-burnt.

But, by a wall with a few kegs, a slender man stood, talking across the bar to a couple of people.

Jon's training kicked in. *Shoulders back, head up and proud,* he told me. *People will believe what they see.*

I walked up to the bar, and conversation stuttered as eyes turned to me. I smiled at them and made my voice as friendly and disarming as possible. "Greetings and salutations," I said. "My name is Chase Galat, and as you can see, I am a traveller." I motioned to my clothes, worn and dirty.

I decided not to pre-empt their questions about what I was and just stick to business. "I am tired and in need of rest. Tomorrow, I will require nourishment and bathing." I paused, hoping for a response, but the man behind the bar simply stared at me. "Do you have any rooms available?"

He looked me up and down, and as he did, I realised I had no money. I had never thought about money with Jon—he had always simply provided it. Delsaran and I had avoided other people on our journey here, so we had never used it. And Greenchapel was small enough to work on favours and reciprocity.

What did I have to trade? There was my armour, I thought. Though damaged, it would be worth a lot of money with the magic D—

I would not sell the armour.

I had my water pouch and clothes, but I would need both of those. That left the Tubelicious. If I wanted to sleep here tonight, I would have to trade it.

The man still stared at me, his hands pressing into the bar. It was now or never.

I pulled out some Tubelicious and put it on the bar. "This," I said, "is Tubelicious. Now, what is Tubelicious, you ask? It is the most delicious ration you've ever had—and nutritionally complete too."

Their silence unnerved me, but I couldn't show that. "Try to live on hardtack and your muscles will weaken and your teeth will fall out." I rapped my fingers on the bar. "But you can get stronger and faster on Tubelicious alone."

I took a piece and ate it. In my dry, anxious mouth, it was a tasteless paste, but I pretended to savour the flavour. "Even better, a small piece will satisfy you like a full meal."

I fought the shaking of my body and forced myself to breathe. I told myself the worst he could say was no, and then I could sleep outside as I had been doing for months.

Still, I felt helpless. I had followed Jon or Delsaran my whole life. And now I was at the mercy of strangers.

Finally, the innkeeper looked down at the Tubelicious on the bar. He picked up a piece and ate it.

"That's good," he said, his eyes widening. Then he looked back at me. "But what are you, exactly?" He was not friendly, but neither was he insulting.

That was a good sign. I didn't have to rely on his goodness—just his self-interest. Jon had told me that, so long ago.

Fools decry greed, claiming financial incentives are evil, Jon said, his voice sharp. *But anyone who has lived in a small town knows people care more about status and power than money. Remove greed, and people do not become saints, but judges. And those who are different are sentenced accordingly.*

Money simply rewards what works. You create something different, and if it makes life better, you profit. Your difference earns status. Jon gave a smug half-smile.

Free societies have free commerce because only commerce rewards society for encouraging people to be who they want to be.

I let the memory pass, and looked into the innkeeper's eyes, coming up with a believable half-lie. "I am Chase Galat, a minotaur," I said. "I am a merchant from a far-off land, but my unfamiliarity with this place left me unprepared for the distance between cities."

"And," the innkeeper said, "you ain't got no money."

"Correct." I let out a breath. "But this Tubelicious is impossible to find anywhere else. And if you have an empty room, you lose nothing by simply letting me sleep in it. The road was bare as I came in, and I have grown accustomed to sleeping on the ground."

The innkeeper grunted. Then he looked down at the Tubelicious and rapped his fingers on the table.

He considered it. That was good. I had him from here—I just needed him to agree to my price. Time to, as Jon would say, put the door in his face.

"Considering how rare and valuable these are, I can offer you a deal that will cost me much more than I paid for them: two for the night and a bath."

The innkeeper laughed. "I have a business to run. I gotta cook hot food for my customers, not feed them rations. What use do I have for this? Give me twenty and you have a deal."

My muzzle made hiding my smile easy. "I understand. Your business is important to you, and these don't really help it. But I need to keep enough to get back on my hooves," I said, and everyone looked down at them. "I can give you five."

"Ten," he responded.

I suppressed a sigh of relief. "Done," I said, then put ten pieces on the counter.

I could sleep in a bed for the first time in months. I needed the rest.

He took the pieces, then handed me a key. "Up the stairs, second door on the left."

"Thank you," I said, and bowed. I made my way up the stairs, their eyes still watching me. Then I unlocked the door and went in.

It was a small room; in Jon's manor, it would be a mere closet. The bed took up the entirety of the far wall, leaving one corner for clothes and a pack, and the other for the chamber pot. Compared to the last few years of my life, though, it was opulence.

I forced myself to remove my woolens before collapsing into bed.

The void came quickly.

Wakefulness came slowly. I became vaguely aware of the shape and weight of my body in my bed. The sheets slid smoothly over my fur, though last night they had not felt nearly as soft. I smelled the yeast of morning bread wafting into my room. The lilt of muffled voices from the street below slipped through my small window. Finally, my eyes fluttered, and saw the light of the sun.

I lay for a while longer, letting myself linger in half-sleep. My body was so sore and stiff, I wondered if I could sleep the day away. But as the sun rose, sleep became more and more impossible, and my thoughts circled subjects I could not handle.

I dressed and exited the room. This early in the morning, the inn was empty, so I wandered around to find the bathing room. Thankfully, it was a small inn, so it wasn't hard.

The room was larger than my own, but not huge. A couple wooden tubs sat against either side, and, on the far wall, a waterspout jutted out of the floor and a basin of clean water hung above the embers of a fire.

I chose the tub closest to the basin and filled it, first with hot water and then with cold. I refilled the basin and hung it back above the fire. Then I stripped naked and got into the tub.

After bathing in rivers for years, I missed the current running over my fur and skin. But I had forgotten how relaxing it was to simply cross my legs and lean back against the wooden slats. I scrubbed myself for a while, then closed my eyes and felt the warm water against my skin.

A couple other people came into the room to bathe, but I paid them no mind. I just wanted to sit there forever, and never deal with my life again.

"Your name is Chase Galat, correct?" I opened my eyes, and a woman stood before me. She was dressed in silk—though not quite as fitted as Jon's—in a practical cut that gave her freedom of movement. Her black hair was short, but lustrously maintained. Behind her stood the innkeeper, looking on anxiously.

I scrambled to grab my clothes, but she waved a hand. "I care not about that. My name is Leidre, and I am the lady of this town, Narasi. I am here about your"—she closed her eyes, concentrating—"Tubelicious." She pronounced it tube-licious, missing the pun. But she held a piece of Tubelicious in her hand, a small bite taken out of it.

My training kicked in again. "I am eager to be of any assistance I can, my lady." My voice was smooth, with a touch of iron inside its deference.

"Where did you get the—"

"Tubelicious," I said gracefully.

"And can I get more?"

I thought she would continue, but she simply crossed her arms and waited. Most people in her position loved to hear themselves talk.

The only place she could get more was Greenchapel. And I knew Delsaran wouldn't have wanted me bringing her there. "I do not think that's possible," I said.

"Is there no way?"

I thought of how much Delsaran loved his independence. Even when the town was under threat. Even when it killed him.

We're made stronger together, Jon had told me.

I took a breath, and a plan formed. Delsaran wouldn't like it, I knew, but he was no longer here. I tried to speak my plan, but my mouth felt like it were far away, and I had no power to open it. I closed my eyes and imagined I were talking to myself. Finally, the words came. "There's a problem."

"There always is," she said.

"The town that grows Tubelicious is under threat from strange magical monsters," I continued. "Void-like black, with a red aura, and all sharp angles."

Leidre raised an eyebrow. "We've dealt with those here but know not what they are."

"We call them nightbringers. In small numbers, they do not pose much of a threat. But the town is small itself."

"I can't afford to send a division of my army to protect it."

I lifted a hand, the water sploshing. "Not necessary. I know the source of these creatures. We stop it, and it's done for good." I tried not to think about our previous attempt to stop it, but I failed. My breath caught in my chest as my lungs closed.

Leidre's eyes widened. She looked at me carefully. "You are an interesting minotaur."

I dipped my head forward in acknowledgement, my muzzle dropping beneath the surface of the water.

"I will agree to eliminate the source of the nightbringers in exchange for these"—she paused for a split-second before pronouncing them correctly—"Tubelicious."

"Thank you," I said. Leidre nodded brusquely, though I noticed the innkeeper behind her breaking into a large smile.

"When will you be ready to leave?" Leidre asked.

"As soon as I get my clothes on," I said. Then I thought of Greenchapel. "A horde of misshapen nightbringers emerged when I was last there. They move slowly on their malformed limbs, but if they find

Greenchapel, I doubt the town would survive."

"I'll grab my mage and a detachment large enough to deal with this threat." Her voice was crisp. "Meet me at the castle in three hours." Then she turned and began to walk away. "Oh," she said, stopping. "How far away is this source?"

"About four days," I said.

"Right," she said. "Provisions, then, too."

She turned and handed a clinking bag to the innkeeper, who opened it and smiled, then she left the room. The innkeeper followed her and left me alone in my now cool tub.

I sat in the bath a moment longer. I felt like I had betrayed Delsaran.

He had given me a family and a home. And now I was going against what he would have wanted. I felt myself shrinking away from my body, as though I were trapped in a corner of my mind.

But I would do whatever I could to protect my home. And that meant I would use every skill I had at my disposal. This problem was too big for me, too big for anyone.

But I could still fix it.

AID

The castle was an old, motte-and-bailey style, not the modern star forts that were popular around Castulo. Its earthworks were rough and simple. The palisade was a single row of unhewn logs, and there was no walk-around; instead, a couple rickety platforms loomed above the wall, from which archers could fire. The motte was high enough, but the keep at its top was little wider than a tower and couldn't be more than three stories tall.

I reached the entrance to the bailey, and the doors opened for me. The enclosed field was large enough for the small army gathered there but had space for little else. The bunkhouse could fit maybe a few hundred troops, and its storehouse could feed them for a month at most. Unless, of course, she had Tubelicious.

Epics are written of soldiers' bravery, but the bravest soldier is nothing without a cook, a smith, a tailor—and accountants to make sure they all get paid. For every soldier here, there were tens of people supporting them. Bakers baked bread and cooks boiled pottage while dried meat, hardtack, cheese, and wine were taken out of storage. Then it was loaded into small carts alongside tents, weapons, and spare uniforms.

I remembered when Jon had found Bri and I playing; Bri had let loose a magical arrow that slaughtered hundreds of demons. Jon, in his obtuse way, offered advice: *The greatest magic is rarely flashy. Grand fireballs can rend armies, but the greatest mage stands impotent before that which changes the very shape of the choices we make.*

I had nodded, my eyes wide in half-feigned attention, then ran off to celebrate the victory with Bri. But now I saw how Tubelicious could change the shape of buildings, travel, and warfare. It wouldn't turn priests of Atar into explorers, but if you were thinking about becoming an explorer, and suddenly rations became cheaper and more delicious . . .

Thinking at the margin, Jon had called it.

Though now those soldiers, cooks, smiths, and tailors all paused to stare at me, taking in my horns and fur.

I stood against the palisade and tried not to think about them. I remembered Bri, looking at me and shouting, *amazing!* I remembered Greenchapel, simply taking me as I was. Maybe I could still be happy there, even without—I dug my hand into my leg.

Leidre emerged from the keep and walked down the steps of the motte. She checked on the progress of everything as she passed by— the readiness of the soldiers, the supplies in the carts, and the heat of the ovens. When there was a problem, she quickly assigned someone to fix it.

Then she came up to me. "Good afternoon, Chase," she said.

"Good afternoon, Leidre." I bowed.

"Feeling rested and ready to go?"

"It was good to sleep in a bed again."

"Good," she said. "And you know your way there? I cannot afford to have my army wait as you search."

"My hooves left deep marks in the wet ground when it rained, and it has not rained since. I—" My body tightened as I thought of my escape from the cavern, running blindly through the dark. My mouth closed up, and speech eluded me.

I closed my eyes and let my breathing calm me. "I was not in a place to remember the last few miles, but I know how to find it again."

"You don't need to tell me what happened," she said, not without compassion. "But you do need to keep it together as you lead us there."

"I will," I said. Then I opened my eyes.

Leidre was already looking around the bailey, judging everything's readiness. A cart wobbled beneath the weight of the supplies packed on it, and she frowned. "If you need anything, find me. I'll be around." Then she strode toward the cart.

I cursed myself softly. I still couldn't think of what had happened. Not even to myself. I wasn't ready to go back. I just wanted to pretend none of this had ever happened.

But then I thought of Hayyan and Andarta in Greenchapel. Delsaran had been so happy to meet Hayyan. I felt his arms around me and Hayyan as he held us. I heard him speak Andarta's name with reverence.

I forced my tight chest to expand with a deep breath. I would do everything that I could for Delsaran's family. Even if it meant facing the nightbringers again. I just had to endure the next few days.

I sat against the wall of the bailey. I looked up at the same sun and remembered my mother's wet breath against my ear, the smile of Bri, and the touch of Delsaran's red beard against my forehead.

"We're ready, Chase," Leidre said, breaking me out of my reverie. "Lead the way."

I walked through the small gate and out of the bailey. The deafening crunch of hundreds of boots on stone followed me. I kept looking back at the rows of soldiers; it was hard to believe that I led them.

We made our way through the town. Children watched the soldiers march past and gawked at the minotaur leading them. We proceeded past the farmer's fields, their crops swaying in the breeze. The road turned to dirt, and wound through the outskirts of the forest, providing a bit of shelter from the sun. Then I found my hoofprint by the side of the road.

I was lucky it had rained when it did, and so heavily. Delsaran had taught me how to track in our long journeys through the woods, but my hoofprints were so clear I might not have needed his lessons.

I looked back, making sure Leidre saw me, then turned into the forest.

The ground had dried, so the carts wound their way through the forest without getting stuck, but the trees still impeded the orderly marching of the army.

I followed the straightest path through the trees, using the sun to keep my direction steady. I watched for the hoofprints that would confirm my direction and could usually find them without difficulty. At times, the forest was so dense that a few steps changed a straight path into a winding mess, and we had to search through the dense foliage to find the next hoofprint. But I had the help of a few other scouts and trackers from the army when I needed it; we always found the trail before the rest of the army caught up.

By nightfall, we had made good progress.

Bedrolls and tents were distributed, and food was consumed. I took a bedroll and some bread and pottage. But I decided to sleep under the stars as Delsaran and I always had.

It felt right.

By the fourth day, I knew we were close. Still, we had seen no trace of the nightbringers. What had happened to them? Normal nightbringers chased whatever was closest—is that what these ones would have done? If so, how come we hadn't seen any? If not, what could compel such a large group to stay together?

Maybe Delsaran had managed to defeat all of them.

I knew it was impossible, but I couldn't stop myself from hoping it.

Whatever had happened to him, we needed to keep moving. This close to the cavern, the ground had been dry when I ran, so there were no hoofprints to follow. I fanned out the scouts, and we moved in a line.

Around noon, I walked into the clearing. Though not as it had been. Now, a path of black, charred vegetation extended out from the middle of the clearing and went deep into the forest.

That meant—

I ran to the centre of the clearing and down the steps. I reached the bottom and sprinted past the kitchen, library, bedroom, and jousting room. Then I hit the next stairs, almost falling over myself trying to reach the bottom. I leapt over my shield and the remnants of my axe, landing on the ground with a grunt.

I looked around quickly. And there he was.

Or what was left of him.

His body had been burned black. His armour had been melted, leaving puddles of dull metal that sunk into his body. His sword, its blade flattened and dull, lay by his side.

I stumbled over to him and fell to my knees. I rolled him over to look at his face, but it was beyond recognition. The only trace of Delsaran was a whisker of red hair. I looked away quickly.

Slavers had taken my family from me. Unjust laws had taken Bri from me. And now, Delsaran had been taken by . . . I wasn't even sure. Nightbringers, we called them, a name devoid of understanding.

I didn't know and it didn't matter. The only thing I knew was that I was cursed.

Cursed to solitude, cursed to fall asleep alone every night, cursed to never feel safe in the love of another. I had always endured whatever conspired against me, no matter how unfair. I thought that, as bad as things were, if I suffered through the pain, they would get better. I would see my mother again, or I'd be friends with Bri forever, or I would have a family with Delsaran.

There are rewards from obedience, the familiar voice intoned.

All I could do was weep.

When I finally stopped crying, I picked up Delsaran's body and sword and carried them up the stairs. I scarcely noticed Leidre, who had been waiting at the top of the stairs, her mage playing with the entertainment room. After I passed, she grabbed her mage by the elbow, and they went down the stairs to study the crystal.

I continued my way up the second set of stairs. I went into the sunshine and found a patch of ground where the grass still grew. Then I lay Delsaran beside it.

I grabbed a shovel from one of the supply carts and waved away a few soldiers who offered to help. Then I began to dig.

It was slow work, and my body was unaccustomed to it. My arms were strong from Delsaran's training, but my back ached. Every time I bent down to lift another shovelful of dirt, I could feel my back protest against the strain. But I kept working.

When the ground came up to my thigh, I stopped. I climbed out of the grave and picked up Delsaran. My back ached, but I gritted my teeth and lowered myself into the grave. I placed Delsaran on the ground and looked at him one more time. I remembered what he had looked like: his red and grey hair, his wide smile, his stocky limbs, his broad shoulders, his thick waist.

Then I reached for the side of the grave and climbed out.

Shovelling the dirt back in was easier. But as I covered more and more of Delsaran, I wanted to believe that, at any moment, his cold body would warm, and he'd cough as his lungs started working again.

I lingered after each shovelful, looking at his body, watching for movement. I knew it was fantasy—he had lain there for days—but I couldn't stop thinking that maybe I was wrong. Maybe his breathing was just too shallow for me to see.

And then his body was completely covered with dirt.

He was gone.

I patted the grave down. Then I took Delsaran's sword and stuck it into the ground. Still, it didn't seem enough. Delsaran had been so full of life. I had to do more.

I pressed my hands against the dirt, trying to will Delsaran's magic into it. I said his mantra. I looked at the felled trees and blue sky, and forced my heart to love them, to take it as the stream to fill my river. I told myself that for all the suffering I had endured, I still had my power to choose.

I recited his mantra one last time, letting the words swell in my chest. Nothing.

I sat there for a while longer, just staring at his grave. Then I walked out of the clearing until I found an acorn, and I planted it in his grave. In that soil, I didn't know if it would grow. But it was the best I could do.

I felt my throat contract and expand, as though words were struggling to escape. Then I opened my muzzle, and they did.

"Thank you, Delsaran, for being my father."

I turned and walked down the stairs.

"He must have had powerful magic to strike such a blow," Leidre's mage said as I arrived, "but he could not have foreseen its consequence. Thankfully, a colleague from Castulo has been asking about magic like this, so I've become familiar."

He picked up one of the books lying on the rune-covered floor. "This crystal is a battery. It absorbed the life-energy from everything around it, and slowly shaped it into nightbringers. His blow released all the energy at once, its safeguards and guides broken. The result?" he asked. "Misshapen masses. Thousands of them."

Leidre chewed on the tip of her index finger. Then she looked at her mage carefully. "If there were a lot of them, where did they go? We encountered none on the way here."

The mage flipped through the book. "I believe," he said, running his finger down a page. "Yes," he resumed, then chewed his lip. "They would have had the ability—no, not *ability*." He read a couple sentences. "They would be compelled toward the largest concentration of sapient life nearby."

Leidre shook her head. "But isn't that Narasi? Then why didn't we see them on the way here. There's nothing else."

I remembered the burned trail I had seen when I entered the clearing. I knew what was in that direction.

"Greenchapel," I said. "They're going to Greenchapel."

RUN

"We leave, now!" Leidre shouted.

People sprang to their feet and gathered what few belongings had been unpacked. I scarcely had time to take a shaft from the supplies and affix it to my axe before we were ready to go.

Then we marched.

Would we reach Greenchapel in time? I didn't know. The misshapen nightbringers moved slowly—but over a full week had passed. How fast were they? I knew I . . . was not in a place to judge their speed when I saw them. If they were even a third as fast as a person, they would be in Greenchapel now, and we wouldn't arrive for another day, at best.

I imagined Greenchapel burned to the ground, and I couldn't shake the image. I tried to focus on my surroundings, on the trees and soldiers around me. But, if Greenchapel burned, Delsaran died for nothing.

Nightfall came earlier than I would have hoped, and I had a hard time laying down to sleep. Even if I saved Greenchapel, would it be my home? Andarta was kind. And she was part of Delsaran's family, just as I was. I remembered Delsaran promising Hayyan they could journey with us. That promise had made me happy.

I watched the stars twinkle. I felt like I did when I was a child, alone and unmoored, scared of what the future would bring.

As my mind groped for anything that would calm it, I thought of Bri. I remembered his smiling face as he looked into my eyes. I heard him screaming "Chase!" as the monsters threatened to overwhelm me. I dreamed of his arms around me as he celebrated his arrow killing the

God-demon.

Could I make new friends like him in Greenchapel? Did I want to? My thoughts blurred into a half-sleep as I got what rest I could.

The next morning, I packed before most soldiers had eaten their breakfast. I gave what help I could to the slowest soldiers and willed everyone to move faster. I folded up tents and wrapped up bedrolls. Then, as I was throwing dirt over the latrine, Leidre came up to me.

"How much further to Greenchapel?" she asked.

"About six leagues," I said.

"We can make that today," Leidre responded. "If we push ourselves."

I nodded and went back to throwing dirt on the latrine.

Leidre walked away, shouting, "Long day today, everyone! Pack the food and water you'll need. We'll be doing a quick march, and the rest of our supplies will catch up tonight or tomorrow. If we don't get there in time, this was all for nothing!"

The morning passed, and the sun beat down overhead. The army stopped for lunch, and everyone brought out the food and water they had carried with them.

I forced myself to eat, bread and pottage going down untasted. I could tell we were getting closer; the grass and shrubs were freshly burnt. But would it be in time?

A few minutes later, we resumed the march.

As the afternoon went on, I began to recognise distinctive trees that Delsaran had taught me about—one forked like a fan, flat and wide; another that had a knot like a face—and knew we were close to Greenchapel.

Up ahead, the grass smouldered. The nightbringers couldn't be far now.

So long as Greenchapel held, we would get there on time.

But would they hold? They were ready for a small force of vaguely human nightbringers, not a horde of misshapen monsters.

I picked up my pace and left the army behind. If I could help Greenchapel hold a minute longer, I would.

Greenchapel was the only home I had left.

The trees cleared, and I looked out on the field of battle.

The last time I had fought the nightbringers in Greenchapel, the trees had funneled them into a stream. Then they were peppered with arrows and dispatched before the next wave reached the fighters.

Andarta and the archers had tried the same strategy—arrows and supernaturally thick vines littered the ground—but the nightbringers had pushed through in a solid mass and spread out over the clearing.

The villagers were fighting for their lives. The barricades were almost useless—as soon as the nightbringers pressed against them, they oozed out along the line. Only the fighters' desperate hacking kept them from being encircled.

But the nightbringers still advanced. The archers had dropped their bows and joined the line, short swords and machetes drawn.

Their steel was a blur, and the black dust of dead nightbringers filled the air. Yet the nearly endless horde of nightbringers still swarmed and pushed everyone back.

I ran.

One of the archers on the edge went down. Andarta glowed white; stalks of grass wrapped around the nightbringers close to the archer. Then she ran in and pulled the archer away.

The line shrank, folding in on itself to prevent the nightbringers from getting around it. The whole line tried to retreat, but as slow as these nightbringers were, they kept pace.

The villagers were going to end up surrounded.

My hooves slammed into the ground as my panting breaths curled around my muzzle. The nightbringers' bodies squeezed together like a solid mass with hundreds of limbs reaching out in every direction. Every time a sword, axe, or spear sliced through one, it seemed to make no difference. There must have been hundreds of nightbringers for each fighter they tried to overwhelm.

I reached the left side of the battle; thankfully, the nightbringers paid me no mind yet. They pushed forward with mindless bloodlust.

I slashed through them, and they turned to dust. But after a couple swings, several jagged lumps of heads twisted, and then a black mass moved toward me. I leaped back from an arm that groped for my ankle.

I hacked through it, but my axe dug into the ground.

I pulled out my axe, but more arms reached toward me, and I had to retreat again.

Could I lead them away and thin the line? No, even if I pulled fifty away, it would scarcely do a thing. The fighters kept retreating, their line folding in on itself.

I ran around the nightbringers and joined the line with a nod to the fighter beside me. Though sleep deprived, I was fresher than the rest of the line, and held my ground. I swung my axe as hard and fast as I could.

My arms burned with each swing, but I knew there was no other option. *Just do what needs doing,* I heard Delsaran say. If we held long enough, Leidre's army would be here.

Then two fighters went down at once. Andarta sprang toward one and sent vines out to protect the other. The vines smoked and blackened, so we rushed to cover the gaps. As I stepped, my axe cut into a nightbringer—but not all the way through. It attacked, and I hopped back. The solid mass of nightbringers pressed in further.

"I can't get them to safety!" I heard Andarta shout. "They're surrounding us!"

"Help is on the way!" I shouted back. "Just keep fighting!"

"Chase?" Hayyan said, but I couldn't make out from where. "What's going—" a grunt cut off their words. I hoped it was from effort, not a wound, but I couldn't afford to look. I just had to trust Andarta to help them if they needed it.

The nightbringers were swarming around me, and I kept falling back. My lungs ached, and I couldn't get enough air. And I was fresh. I could see the other fighters out of the corner of my eye, their swings slowing and the nightbringers forcing them further and further back.

If the nightbringers pressed us on both sides, there was no way we would survive.

My eyes barely registered the shapes of the nightbringers as I swung. Black limbs and red light flashed before me, cut in two by my silver axe.

Then something hit me from behind. I spared a glance back, and it was a fighter, falling back from the onslaught of nightbringers; the other side of the line had collapsed back upon us.

We had been closed in.

The fighter turned as well, shock on his face as he realised what had happened. Then he screamed as a black limb struck his leg; the flesh reddened, then turned black. He swung his sword at it weakly, and managed to sever the limb, but he had already begun to topple.

He hit the ground, hard.

I hooked my axe into his armour and yanked him into the small space in the middle of our circle; he sprawled onto the ground, his sword flung away from him. Screaming, he held his leg.

I held my ground. I dropped my shield and put everything I had into each swing. I tried to hold our circle together. But with the gap beside me, I couldn't cleave wide enough. Black limbs scorched my legs, and I gritted my teeth against the pain. Each time they hit me, my flesh charred more before I could cut them in two. I wouldn't last much longer.

Then a spear slid past my right leg and severed two limbs coming toward me, and another fighter stepped in beside me. Their spear flashed in dark hands, and out of the corner of my eye I could see their face: Hayyan.

I lowed and planted my hooves. We would do this together.

I swung my axe wide and hacked through swaths of them while Hayyan's spear darted out to chop off any limbs that snuck beneath my arc. I laughed, deep and hearty. My legs burned, my lungs ached, and my arms had been charred. But I didn't care. With Hayyan here, I could fight forever.

A gust of cold air whipped by, sublimating into ice in front of me, and the nightbringers turned to dust. I looked up, and on the other side of the nightbringers, the soldiers from Leidre's army had arrived. Behind them, the mage, his arms raised, guided the wind and ice.

"They're here!" I shouted. The army charged into the mass of nightbringers.

The nightbringers ignored the threat behind them until swaths had already been reduced to dust. When they finally turned, they left their backs open to me. I hacked through them and saw Hayyan do the same.

Within minutes, the nightbringers were dispatched, floating away on the wind.

Hayyan and I collapsed against each other, panting for breath. My arms felt like lead; I could only imagine what Hayyan's felt like.

Most of the people of Greenchapel collapsed wherever they were, too. Weary smiles covered their faces.

Andarta hobbled around, using her staff for balance as she checked on the wounded. She went to those who had fallen and tended to them: she cleaned their burns with a little bottle, then bandaged what she could before she pressed her glowing hand against the wounds.

Occasionally, Andarta would look suspiciously at Leidre and the soldiers before pointedly ignoring them and cleaning another wound.

Leidre spent some time looking at Greenchapel. She examined its ramshackle houses and mismatched people. I could see some confusion in her eyes; I imagined her wondering how a poor little village like this could have developed Tubelicious—and still be so poor. But, like Andarta, Leidre did not waste much time on these thoughts: she soon turned to her soldiers. They were well-trained but didn't have the experience with the nightbringers that the people of Greenchapel did, so a few had suffered serious injury. She directed the medics to the soldiers who needed aid and ensured no one was missed.

"So," Hayyan said, taking a break to breathe after the one word, "what the Krek happened?"

How could I explain everything that had happened? I could barely think about it. They deserved to know. But I couldn't even open my mouth.

Thankfully, Leidre came up to me then, her soldiers all cared for.

"My mage tells me that there might be a few more groups of nightbringers throughout this forest, but that no new groups will form," she said, looking down at me. "He's going to send everything he learned to some colleagues in Castulo. Hopefully, it'll prevent any future mage from losing control of magic like this."

I nodded but remained silent. Hayyan looked at her, their eyes wide.

"So, this is Greenchapel," Leidre said. She smiled at the houses in the distance. It was a cunning smile, though it had warmth to it, too. "I had heard rumours of a village somewhere in these forests, filled with refugees. I'm glad it's been successful."

She looked back at me. "I will trade fairly with them—I'm no raubritter who takes the work of others. After all, if I can demonstrate my trustworthiness, they'll likely come to me with any future inventions. But this has been an expensive endeavour for me. Our trip to Greenchapel added a few days to our campaign, and our supplies run low."

I worked my way to my feet, careful not to strain my too-tired muscles. "Leidre," I said, "this is Hayyan." I motioned to them. "They are the child of the founder of Greenchapel, and a formidable warrior in their own right."

Hayyan pushed the butt of their spear into the ground, then used it to lift themselves to their feet. They had a harder time than I did.

"Hayyan," I said, "this is Leidre. She is the skilled and conscientious leader of Narasi, a city about six days' journey from here. She's eager to find a way to trade with Greenchapel."

Hayyan nodded. "It's good to meet you," they said. "I'm Hayyan."

They approached each other to shake hands. Leidre sized Hayyan up quickly, taking in their wiry and lithe body, and, despite the awkwardness there, their quick and intelligent eyes. Hayyan, however, looked a bit like a housecat stalking out a new piece of furniture: careful, curious, and mystified at the same time.

"What's Narasi like?" Hayyan asked. "Does it have a castle?"

Leirdre smiled. "It does. Though not as grand a castle as you may find in the larger cities. It's an older, motte-and-bailey castle."

Hayyan tilted their head. "I've never heard of—"

"Where's Del?" Andarta asked as she approached.

My body stiffened.

"Chase?" she said, watching me. "What's wrong?"

"Mom," Hayyan said, their voice low. "He's not here."

Leidre's eyes went between us quickly. "If he was the man accompanying Chase," she said, and, with great effort, I nodded, "he fought the nightbringers in their lair, and almost destroyed them. He must have been brave and strong."

Andarta gripped her staff, her knuckles turning white. Hayyan's legs gave out; they landed on their ass and cried. Hayyan's sobs spurred Andarta into action, and she held them tight.

Andarta saw me staring, and said, "Chase, come here." I dutifully obeyed, and she wrapped me in her arms too.

And despite all the tears I had already shed, I cried again. I cried because I was so alone. And cried because I was not.

When the tears passed, Andarta said, "Welcome to Greenchapel." She forced a smile and stuck out her hand, but her eyes watched Leidre warily. "My name is Andarta."

Leidre took her hand and shook it firmly. "I'm Leidre," she said, "Lady of Narasi."

Andarta looked over Leidre's army, which still tended wounds and checked equipment. "Narasi seems to have grown since I was last there. It must be well governed." Her voice was clipped, but sincere.

"I can't take too much credit. Most of the job is backing off and letting people do what they know best," she said. Then her lip twitched. "While paying close enough attention that you know exactly when to step in."

Andarta chuckled, her eyes narrow. "And what led you to step in here?"

Leidre brushed her short bangs back. "Chase showed me the Tubelicious, and thought that, in exchange for my help with the nightbringers, we could come to some sort of agreement. A portion of your crop each year would be a boon to me."

Andarta's bottom lip twisted. I had known she wouldn't like it. But she was also practical: without Leirdre, she wouldn't have survived, and they both knew it.

"I appreciate the help with the nightbringers," she said. "But there was no agreement in place before it. I cannot hold myself hostage to what you want simply because you saved my life."

"I wouldn't want to hold you hostage," Leidre said. "But I don't think you realise how generous I'm being. By law, this land belongs to me. I am willing to look the other way on that. In exchange, all I ask is that you send me Tubelicious each harvest."

Andarta's brow tightened, and her muscles flexed. She looked over the villagers, still sitting on the grass. Her back straightened.

This was going all wrong. They both wanted to be reasonable, but Leidre knew she had power. And Andarta had founded Greenchapel to avoid the power of others. Then I remembered something Jon had told me so long ago.

To negotiate, show your opposite that you want the deal as much as they do. Listen to their concerns, and then communicate yours as problems to be solved together. They will devote their intelligence to making a better deal for you.

Love may bind us to friends, but self-interest binds us to strangers.

Andarta opened her mouth to speak, but I spoke first. "Leidre, Andarta appreciates what you have done. But she came out here to be independent. Demanding a yearly tax ties her to you in a way she cannot bear.

"Andarta," I continued, "Leidre does not want you under her control. But she spent many resources coming out here and owes it to the people of Narasi not to come back empty handed." I took a quick breath and closed my eyes.

"Leidre, how would you like to control Tubelicious yourself? Andarta can show you how to sow and grow the Tubelicious. You can take full credit for it. In return, you agree to respect Greenchapel's independence, and never acknowledge its existence."

I opened my eyes, and Andarta nodded. I breathed and looked over to Leidre. Her head rested against her hand as she considered the deal.

At least she was thinking, I told myself. We were moving toward a solution instead of digging in deeper.

Finally, Leidre asked, "What's the yield of Tubelicious?"

"About a thousand bushels per acre," Andarta responded.

Leidre's eyes widened before she got her face under control. She knew she had tipped her hand, and she smiled, confident and sheepish at the same time. "That would be an acceptable compromise."

Andarta nodded. "Then it's a deal."

They shook hands.

"I look forward to working with you," Leidre said.

"It'll be fun," Andarta responded.

They held each other's hands for a moment longer before they let it drop, and Leidre said, "Well, then, I must ready my troops for departure."

"How long will that take?" Andarta asked.

"Our supplies arrive later tonight, so we'll leave at dawn."

Andarta paused. "I can be ready to go then. We'll need to plant this quickly to get you harvesting by fall."

Leidre smiled. "I look forward to your company," she said, then they both walked away.

Once they had gone far enough, I sat down next to Hayyan, exhausted.

"I don't think I've ever seen my mom agree to something she didn't already want to do," Hayyan said. They looked at me, impressed. "I've never managed it, anyway."

"I learned a lot about negotiation as a child," I said. I thought of Jon, my feelings more mixed than ever. Having found a family, I could forgive him even less for taking me from mine. But I also remembered him willing to do whatever it took to save my life. I understood the depth of feeling beneath his oblivious aloofness.

And now here I was, using his tactics for the people I cared about.

His tactics, yes, but he would never have leaped in just because he was there. I had learned that from Delsaran.

For all my life, I had followed one, then the other. I had aped their manners and imbibed their beliefs.

Now, I stood not in their shadows, but on their shoulders.

"I am Chase," I told myself. I had said it a million times, introducing myself to people. It was time to introduce me to myself.

Delsaran had been right. We hoard gold while we squander our heart. Most of my life, I had access to incredible wealth, but it was in Delsaran's arms that I first felt alive. What is the point of wealth, if it strips from us everything that makes life worth living? If we are mere cogs in the machine of progress, then the only place we can stand with our soul intact is upon its ruins.

And yet, Jon had been right, too. Those who say money is not important have never had empty pockets while they faced their starving child. People will do whatever it takes to protect their family, including, if needed, deceit and betrayal. How can you trust people like that? You make it in their interest to work with you. Take out self-interest, and we become not saints, but warring clans, unwilling to cooperate with those we do not deem part of our tight-knit family.

I couldn't see how they fit together. But I knew where I needed to go to find my answer.

"I'm going back to Castulo," I said.

Hayyan opened their mouth, then saw the look in my eyes. They smiled. "Want a travelling companion?"

I laughed and hugged them. "Of course."

There was so much planning to do. We would have to talk to Andarta before she left. We would have to pack. And we would have to do so much more I hadn't even thought of yet. But there was one thing I knew:

I would see Bri again.

IV

HOME

Hayyan and I hiked through forest and field, over hill and around swamp. But this time, I did not avoid towns.

I would not hide again.

Each town greeted me with whispers and stares, and I clutched my axe, ready to defend myself. But they just wanted to know what I was. No one had heard of the minotaur named Chase.

Through the first part of our journey, we had no money and few skills that could earn some, so we passed through towns quickly. We could have laboured for food and lodging but the next day we still would have foraged and slept on the road.

When harvest season came, we would stop for a few days and earn a bit of gold. Hayyan loved these days. As the sun set and our work finished, they would spend hours in the tavern, talking to everyone.

"What's it like, being a farmer?" they would ask. The farmer would stare at them, knowing Hayyan had just spent all day working in the field. But Hayyan, undeterred, would ask another question. "Have you ever lived anywhere else?"

Castles were especially exciting to Hayyan: grandiose structures on a scale they could hardly believe. Every time we passed one, Hayyan would examine the walls, keeps, and turrets, and ask locals what it looked like on the inside. I wondered what they would have thought of Jon's old manor, knowing I had lived in it.

As the season went on, I told them stories of my life there. How I had played with Bri through the woods, how Jon could be so brilliant and so obtuse at the same time. How the cook would wake early to bake bread and pastries, and always had extra ready in case we were suddenly visited by any dignitary from a far-off land.

"How would you do anything other than eat?" they asked.

I laughed and said, "Well, soon you'll get to see for yourself." Because I recognised these woods. I saw the stream, looking so much smaller now, where Bri and I had faced thousands of demons. I saw the clearing where I—there was no point denying it—had killed Rorvin and set my journey to Greenchapel in motion. I knew in just a few more steps, we would emerge from the forest and see my childhood home, reborn.

But when we stepped through the trees, we saw only its skeleton.

The frame dwarfed me as I approached it. Beams, greyed from the weather and smelling of must, towered into the sky. Far above, the joists of its roof stood like ribs.

"I don't understand," I said.

Hayyan walked up to the beams. They studied them, then said, "This isn't that old. If you look at the ends of the beams, there aren't many checks—the wood is still intact. It's probably been less than a year. Do you think they could still be building it?"

I looked around and saw nothing but grass and trees. "No," I said. "If they were still building it, there would be supplies everywhere."

My hand dug into my thigh. Hayyan noticed it, and held me, their arms warm against my fur. "Do you have any idea what could have happened?" they asked.

I shook my head. "Jon had money in everything; nothing short of the whole continent going under could have bankrupted him. That leaves him deciding not to build it, or something happening to him." Then I remembered what Hayyan said earlier. "But why would he have waited so long to begin construction?"

I stood there, just staring at the grey wood.

Hayyan broke their hug and looked around. "I grew up in the forest. I'll look for clues," they said.

We walked around the clearing while Hayyan examined the grass and trees. Delsaran had taught me about tracking, but Jon had taught me to respect other people's expertise.

That was confirmed when Hayyan pointed at a patch of grass I had just looked past. "It's almost a perfect square," they said. "That's not natural."

I had to study it before I understood what they meant. Most of the clearing was covered by grass, with occasional weeds pushing through. But where they pointed, the grass and weeds mixed. At some point, much of that grass had died.

"Probably a tent," I said. "To shelter the supplies from the elements." I moved the weeds aside with my axe. "I don't see any scraps of it, so it was taken away."

We looked for any other clues. We walked around the frame of the house and the edge of the clearing but found nothing.

"There's no tools or materials forgotten," I said, my voice flat. "This wasn't a panicked exit. These workers chose to leave and were never replaced."

Hayyan nodded slowly at my words. "What does that mean?" they asked.

"It means that whatever caused this didn't happen here," I said. "The workers heard about it and left."

Hayyan wrapped their arms around me once more. "I'm sorry, Chase," they whispered. After days on the road, they smelled like ripened cheese, but I was comforted by their presence. "What do we do now?" they asked.

"I don't know," I said. I had not planned further than seeing Bri and Jon again.

I broke the hug, then breathed in deep. I smelled the grass I had spent hours lying in, the flowers Bri and I had trampled through, and the distant brook I drank from. I felt comforted by the memories, even as part of me felt like a helpless, subservient child once again. Without Bri, could I confront a society that still saw me as less than a person?

"I wish Jon or Delsaran were here to tell me what to do," I said. "I came here to become my own person, but right now I just crave the certainty they both projected. I feel lost without it."

Hayyan looked down at the grass. "I never knew Del as well as you, and Mom couldn't have chosen anyone better to be my uncle. But he was just a person."

"I know." I stared up at the sky, where the sun still rose. "I see his mistakes now—and Jon's. But I see mistakes in every decision I could make, too. If we enter Castulo, eventually someone will recognise me, and the fiction of my death will be revealed. They'll still want me for killing Rorvin." I sighed. "But if we don't go into Castulo, we're much less likely to find any leads, even if Jon and Bri left the city."

"Could I enter Castulo for you?"

I looked into Hayyan's soft, dark eyes. "It's so much bigger than anywhere you've been before. I doubt you would even know where to start."

Hayyan sat down on the grass. "Chase, sometimes you just need to do what needs doing. I want to see Castulo, but I came here to help you. Whatever you decide, I'm in."

"I'm sorry," I said. "It's easy to see others' mistakes. It's hard to see our own. Now I understand those who proclaim they're always right even as they destroy their own lives—ignoring reality is less painful than dealing with our flaws."

Hayyan snorted. "Mom always says that. And then proceeds to point out my flaws, not her own."

I laughed and sat down beside Hayyan. They were my family now, and I took strength from that. I breathed and let some of the tension out of me.

They were right. I wanted to find Bri. And, as dangerous as it was, only one path gave me good odds of finding him.

With more determination than I felt, I said, "Ready your spear. Because we're going to Castulo."

Hayyan admired Castulo's large white spires, which towered above the squat slums that surrounded the city. Even at this distance, I felt so small in comparison. In Greenchapel, it seemed like I could forge my own fate, and stand tall. Here, I could spend my whole life building a tower and it would be nothing but a stunted shack compared to the grand spires of Castulo.

"So, how are we going to do this?" Hayyan asked.

"Jon faked my death before I left, and it looks like he succeeded. No one has been looking for me. Still, I can't wander around aimlessly—someone would recognise me eventually."

"So, we need to find your friends fast."

I nodded. "But they may not even be in Castulo. Jon's business partners might know where they are, or at least where Jon is. They liked me, and always spoke of my eloquence and composure, but many are also the type who . . ." I gazed into Hayyan's eyes. "They might not see me as more than what I legally am."

"I still don't understand how anyone can think like that." They shook their head, then their eyes widened. "Wait, what about Del's friends?"

"They would help me, but I don't know who they were or how to find them."

Hayyan sighed. "Not knowing is strange to me. Greenchapel runs on gossip."

"Gossip," I said. "That's it. Everyone knew who the richest man in Castulo was, and whatever happened to him would be the talk of the city."

"Then we just need to find people who wouldn't know you're a wanted minotaur."

I thought about who would be least likely to know of me. "I doubt anyone in the slums would be connected to the government. We can ask around there without much risk."

Hayyan squeezed my arm. "And if anything goes wrong?" they asked.

"I hope you're good at running."

"I did not expect to see so much poverty here," Hayyan said. They looked over sun-dried mudbricks and coarsely thatched roofs that were scarcely large enough to fit a lying form.

"The slums of Castulo have expanded in the years I've been away," I said.

"How can they have so much wealth and so much poverty?"

"Jon said progress is the best way to fight poverty. The poor of today live better than the merchants of the past."

"And yet, these people are poorer than we were in Greenchapel." Hayyan smacked the butt of their spear into the dirt.

"Back when farmers left their fields fallow, these people likely worked on farms that scarcely grew enough to feed them," I said. "Then druids bred alsike to feed livestock while fertilizing soil, and wizards developed cryomantic carts to bring food to market—and farmers owned their land so they'd profit from investing—and . . . we didn't need as many farmers."

"Where did that wealth go?" Hayyan asked.

"What?"

"The farms are producing more than before. So how do these people have less?"

I studied Hayyan's gentle eyes. "I've never thought about it that way. There are more healers, artisans, and scholars who work to make life longer and easier in the future. Jon would say, what are our lives compared to the billions that will come?"

"Mom would never have allowed such riches beside such squalor."

"It feels wrong to me, too," I said. "Without that growth, Leidre wouldn't have had an army to save Greenchapel. There are always trade-offs. But if the future will be better, then those who need the help most are here today."

Hayyan touched my arm. "Either way, right now we need to ask someone for help." They motioned toward a woman who smushed mud into straw and set the bricks out to dry in the sun.

I walked up to her; when she noticed me, she jumped, then retreated a few steps.

"Greetings," I intoned. "I am Chase—" I cut myself off just before saying Galat. "I am new to Castulo." I motioned to the city with an elegant flourish of my arm. "I have come to ask you a few questions, if I may."

"I don't want any trouble," she said. Her eyes went to my axe and Hayyan's spear.

I sighed. I had spoken like Jon. I remembered how lonely his words left me. And I remembered how Delsaran had teased me about it.

The right words, Delsaran had said, *are those that connect you to another.*

"Sorry," I said to the woman. "Let me start again." I took a breath. "My name's Chase. I'm looking for my friend, but he's gone missing. He's a bit famous, so I was hoping that you've heard of him."

She seemed to relax a bit. "Your friend's name?" she asked.

"Jon Galat."

Her eyes darted toward the city. "If he's your friend," she said, "you're too late." She motioned to the shacks around her. "Some here used to work for him. Jobs hard to come by since he left."

My mouth went dry, and I had to work some saliva into it to ask my next question. "What happened to him?"

"Don't know. Ran afoul of someone he shouldn't have, I think." She paused, and my hand gripped my thigh. "A lot of people said it didn't happen right."

Hayyan's hand stroked my back. Their fingers pressed against me but failed to sink into my rigid flesh.

Hayyan stepped in, and asked, "Do you know what happened to his friends? Brimark, Marcus, and . . ."

"Avinna," I managed to finish.

The woman pursed her lips. "Never heard those names before," she said. "Heard some people fought for him. They're in jail now."

"Thank you so much," Hayyan said. They pressed a coin into her hand, and she slipped it into her pocket. "If your words help us save his friend, we will be grateful."

We stepped away and let her get back to making bricks. She seemed a bit more energized doing it, shaping the bricks more square.

I tried to get control over myself as we walked. I had expected hardship coming back. I had expected a fight for my very existence, with Bri leading the charge.

I had not expected a fight to save him.

"How are you doing, Chase?" Hayyan asked, their voice soft and gentle.

I took a big breath. I smelled the mud and my unwashed fur, and felt the sun warm me. It's the same sun, I heard my mother say, and I drew strength from that. The same sun that shone upon Delsaran, Jon, Bri, Hayyan, Andarta, Avinna, and Marcus.

I breathed out, then I gazed into Hayyan's eyes.

"I'm ready to fight for my family," I said.

PLAN

Dusk approached, and the moon rose above the horizon. It was time to go.

Even at night, Castulo was too busy for the streets to be abandoned, and I drew stares and whispers. But I had decided not to hide. There was no way I could cover my horns and pass for human, anyway.

Hayyan followed me through the slums and past the sprawling shops and factories to the city walls. They stood in awe of those walls, towering above them.

The walls had been built hundreds of years ago, back when the city was nothing but a few tradespeople, nobles, and a market. As former farmers moved in, Castulo grew in wealth, and the city expanded well beyond its walls. Now, they enclosed little more than the market and government buildings—including the jail.

The gate had a single guard watching the flow of traffic. She would spot me, I knew, and my breath caught. Still, I should be safe. There had been no manhunt for me, so the guards hadn't been involved. And I had made my choice knowing the risks.

The arch of the gate towered above me as I walked beneath it, right beside the guard. She would only need to take a few steps and reach out to grab me.

And then we were through. I looked back, and the guard had already moved on to study those coming in behind me.

I let out the breath I was holding and studied the old city centre. Its ornate government buildings and marble offices of old money and vested power had changed little. However, right by the marketplace, in almost the centre of the city, a new spire reached high into the sky.

Something about it rubbed me the wrong way, but I couldn't say what. It just felt wrong.

But I had no time to consider urban planning. I walked briskly to the prison, built into the side of the wall.

It was less impressive than I remembered. Its walls were tall enough that I couldn't climb over them, but they did not tower over me like they used to. The building itself was squat and grey, with few windows or doors. Its dreariness would only be surpassed by the lives of those who lived in it.

They called it the separate system, I had read: prisoners were supposed to face themselves and the error of their ways, so they were kept silent and isolated. They even wore shutters over their face so they could see nothing but the ground in front of them.

I tried to imagine Bri in one of those, even more lonely than I had been for most of my life. "I've got to save Bri," I whispered to Hayyan.

"What do we do?"

"First we have to find out if he's in there. I might be able to find out through the council, but I would be recognised there. There's no way I could blend into the prison population. And if we broke into the prison and he's not there . . ."

Hayyan stroked my arm gently as I trailed off. "This is just so wrong." They looked at the silhouettes of the grand buildings in the darkness. "Such splendor and wealth, and yet you can't even do what's right. Instead, there are laws."

"Delsaran told me something similar, once," I said. "People turn customs and laws into dogma, and force people to fit into a society that does not work for them. Rules don't solve problems; people with the courage to do what is right do.

"But Jon taught me the opposite truth: some problems are too big to be solved by anything less than a society working together. But that involves trusting people you'll never talk to again. Laws must apply to everyone, every time, or else trust becomes impossible.

"They're both right, and they're both wrong." I sighed. "I feel like every time I think I've found a truth, it cracks, and I catch the merest glimpse of the greater truth far behind it."

"Mom was always happy with her truths." Hayyan leaned against the prison wall. "But I always felt her truths didn't explain everything, yet I didn't have the experience or knowledge to say why." They laughed. "So, I was a bit of a brat when I was younger, frustrated for reasons I couldn't express. That's why I needed to get away."

"I've learned so much, too. But part of me still wants someone else to make the decision. If this goes wrong, it's on my shoulders."

"I get that, but people slip and die after making the decision to bathe," Hayyan said. "At some point, you just have to set your eyes on the horizon and keep walking."

I laughed, though it was laced with bitterness. They were right, I knew, but I had seen the consequences of those bad decisions in a way they had not.

"I'll stand by you, whatever you decide. You're not doing this alone," Hayyan said.

I took a shuddering breath. "Thank you," I whispered.

Then Hayyan and I jumped as a voice called out, "I never expected to see you again, Chase."

I gripped my axe and looked behind me but couldn't find the source of the voice.

Then something crunched above me, and I saw a dark shape climb down a building close to us. It jumped the last few feet, landing in a crouch before straightening out into a lanky shape. Their face was hidden beneath their dark cloak, but two sinewy hands reached up and pulled the cloak back.

The long face of Marcus emerged from the darkness.

"Marcus," I breathed. "I can't believe it's you."

"It's good to see you, Chase," he said. "You'll have to tell me how you're still alive. But first, who's your companion?"

"Marcus, this is Hayyan. They're Delsaran's child. Hayyan, this is Marcus, Bri's dad."

"Pleasure to meet you," Hayyan said and put out their hand.

Marcus took it. "Delsaran's child? Well, the pleasure's all mine." He turned to me. "I assume Delsaran has something to do with your continued existence?"

"He helped me leave Castulo after Jon faked my death."

"Of course, the fire." Marcus said. "I always wondered—"

"What happened here?" I interrupted. "I arrived to find the manor a skeleton, and heard rumours that Jon is gone."

Marcus looked toward the prison. "It wasn't right." His voice was quiet, yet deep. "Bri, Avinna, and I fought to protect him. But I don't think we understood how messed up things had become." He shook his head. "Sorry. Let me start at the beginning." He took a breath. "About a year after you died, Jon left Castulo, and he didn't say where he was going.

"A few months ago, we received a letter from him. He said he was coming back, and we should meet him at the Alucan Crossroad, about three days out of Castulo. And that work should begin on his new estate. But when Jon arrived, golems attacked." He spat. "Avinna held them off until her sword shattered and her shield split. Brimark charged in to help her."

He looked into the sky. "I knew it was hopeless and I would have to save them later. So, I ran. And I've been planning to break them out since." His voice quavered.

"I understand," I said. "I—" I swallowed, then took a breath to steady myself. "I ran when Delsaran died. I tried to get to him, but I couldn't, and it was either run or die in vain." I felt the hot tears welling, even after months had passed.

Hayyan held me, and after a moment Marcus joined the hug.

But I couldn't stop thinking about Bri. "Is Bri here, then?" I asked.

"And Avinna," Marcus said. Then he smiled. "I had an idea to break them out, but I needed a distraction. Someone who'd stand out. Who'd look big and scary and make them pay attention."

"Right," I said. "Some of Delsaran's friends might be capable of that. But I don't know how to find them."

An elbow poked me in the ribs. "He means you," Hayyan said.

"Oh." Marcus had towered over me when I met him so many years ago; only now did I realise I was looking down at him.

Marcus chuckled. "That'll give me and Hayyan time to free Bri and Avinna. Then we can cover you while you make your escape."

Hayyan studied Marcus's thick forearms and massive shoulders that swallowed his neck. "I'm a decent shot. I can help."

"Excellent. I've got a cache of blunt arrows—so long as we don't hit an eye, it should keep us from killing anyone. I've got a bow for Bri as well—he's as good an archer as I am."

"So, how exactly are we going to do this?" I asked Marcus.

"Every day, the prisoners beg Atar to change them into good members of society. It's one of the only times they're let out of the main compound," he said. "They do it in small shifts to prevent the prisoners from being able to whisper to each other. So, we'll be able to grab Bri and Avinna easily."

Marcus motioned to the top of the building he had climbed down from. "I'll perch up there, and signal when Bri and Avinna leave the chapel. Then we'll blow the wall open."

Hayyan and I shared an incredulous look. "Trust me," Marcus said. "I've got some clay enchanted with a shatter spell—it'll break a hole in the wall so big you could bring a chariot through."

I laughed. "Then what do I do?"

"You'll charge in and lead away as many guards as you can. Hayyan and I will free Brimark and Avinna then cover your return to the hole with our arrows."

"So, I've got the hardest job," I said. I felt a pressure rise in my throat and chided myself for it. I had told myself that I was willing to risk myself to save Bri. I tried to think of another plan that could work. A battle would overwhelm us. Politics would expose me. We had no mage, and no money to bribe a guard. It was Marcus's plan, or no plan.

"I'm trusting you, Chase," said Marcus.

"I'll do it for Bri," I said. I tried to sound as brave as I could, but Hayyan's hand brushed against my arm reassuringly.

"Excellent." Marcus smiled. "Then we have to get them—and us—to safety. I have a safehouse near here, but all the prisoners look gaunt. I doubt they've been fed well. So, we'll need to set up a trap to slow the guards."

"I grew up trapping animals," Hayyan said. "Leave that to me."

"Perfect," Marcus said. "Then let's go back to my safehouse so we can gather everything."

We followed Marcus through the streets, and I struggled to pay attention to the route, though I knew I'd need it. Instead, I remembered what all the constables had said about me, so long ago: I was wild, and couldn't live in society; I needed to be put down.

Now, I would have to act as though they were right. I would have to be fearsome. Feral. I felt shame, fear, and guilt.

But a thought cut through everything and cleared my mind:

I will save my family.

BOOM

I waited in the dark shadow of the prison, looking up at the stars. They were so dim I could barely make out several that had shone bright while I travelled with Delsaran. Still, the night was dark. Hayyan was a mere silhouette, standing back from the wall, waiting. Marcus I couldn't see; even the building he waited behind was almost invisible. I only knew where it was from the stars it blocked out.

I looked at the clay, stuck against the wall. I just needed to tap it and say the magic word, "Effusee," and it would go off. Then I just had to run through the hole and distract all the guards.

Yeah, easy.

I had discarded my cloak, leaving my breastplate to gleam in the moonlight. Marcus had applied some paint on it, brown, green, and red, highlighting the bulbous patches from my battles with the night-bringers and the rust from my time in the forest. But he had left the polished steel exposed enough to shine. *It'll make you look scarier*, he had said. Then he put more red on my axe.

I shifted my weight from one hoof to the other and bent over to stretch my back. I twisted from side to side. I leaned against the wall, picked at my teeth, and then checked my axe and shield for nicks.

That must have occupied at least a few minutes, I thought. I opened and closed my hands against my axe and shield, repeating the magic word as I did so. "Effusee, effusee, effusee."

Part of me wanted Marcus to call out now, and part of me wanted him to never call out. I just needed—

"Now!" Marcus whisper-shouted.

I reached for the clay with my shield hand, and my shield covered it, blocking my hand. Cursing myself, I smacked my axe hand against the clay, shouted, "Effusee," then stepped back.

A cloud of dust enveloped me as the spell went off, and the world went black. The dust was sharp against my tongue. Bricks clattered to the ground as their support disintegrated.

I had to be fast to catch them off-guard, so I moved through the dust cloud toward the clattering bricks, my hand brushing against the wall until I found the hole.

I tried to bellow as I ran through the dust but ended up choking on it instead. My charge turned into a stumble, and I fought to stay upright.

I escaped the dust cloud and emerged into the yard, lit by a few enchanted lights. Straight ahead, the prisoners were chained in a row, walking back from the chapel. I wanted to check for Bri and Avinna, but I forced myself to look into the yard. Staying on task was the only way to save them.

A half-dozen guards were on my left, ahead of the prisoners. Wearing red shirts with a blue sash, they inched toward me, clubs drawn. They all had the same look of confusion and apprehension on their faces. They didn't know what to make of me, but they knew I wasn't supposed to be there.

I coughed out the last of the dust, raised my axe into the air, and bellowed. I glared into the eyes of the guards.

I charged.

Most guards jumped back, and I ran past them, but one stood his ground and stared me down. If I took him out, the others might panic and keep their distance from me long enough for Hayyan and Marcus to rescue Bri and Avinna.

Axe high, I charged straight for him, snarling as best I could. I swung my axe in a circle above my head. He raised his club to parry it. Only when I got in too close to swing did his eyes dart to my shield; they widened as I smashed into him and sent him sprawling to the ground.

I lowed.

Then, before the guards could react, I ran deeper into the prison yard.

I glanced back. Almost all of them ran after me as fast as they could, clubs out. One stayed behind to help the guard I had knocked over, but neither of them looked back toward the hole where Hayyan and Marcus ran toward the line of prisoners. I forced myself to look away— I didn't want the guards to think there was anything important behind me.

Ahead of me, I could see another guard post with four guards. Three had their clubs drawn, but one had a short bow out, and, judging from her shoulders, she knew how to use it. I tried to charge her, but the other guards stepped between us, their clubs raised.

I lifted my shield and blocked their blows as I shouldered through them. But the archer loosed her arrow.

It plinged against my breastplate. The short bow was meant for prisoners and could not pierce my armour.

The guards tried to get around my shield and swung for my arms and legs. In the tight quarters, they had no space to build up their power, but their blows still stung, and I gritted my teeth against the pain.

But I had to keep moving; if the guards caught me, everything would fail.

A few blows rained down on my arms and legs as I coiled my body, then smashed my shield into the guard in front of me. He didn't go flying like the first, but he stumbled enough that I could sprint past him.

My legs and arms were stiff from the beating they had received, and every step jarred them. I struggled to stay ahead of the guards. And I knew my arms would not be much use in another fight.

I heard the twang of the arrow a split second before it bounced off my shoulder blade; though my armour held, I stumbled forward. Another club struck my arm, and it went numb before I managed to keep running.

I zigzagged to avoid the arrows, but the guards were too close behind me; one swung his club and struck my horns, wrenching my neck. I lurched to the side as an arrow whizzed by me, then desperately flailed my shield with the little strength I had left. Two blows hit my shield, but another cracked against my ribs. Even with my breastplate, I gasped, air rushing out of my lungs.

I tried to keep running, but my hooves landed heavy on the ground as I gulped down air. Instead, I leaned forward and had my legs catch me.

Then, around the corner of the building, at least eight more guards arrived. They dressed like the others but held swords and shields. There was no way I could smash through all of them. I needed to head back now, or I never would.

But as I turned, a club swung for my head. I tried to catch the club on my horns, but my wrenched neck wouldn't move. I closed my eyes and prepared for the head blow that would end me.

The guard screamed. The club dropped from his hands as he clutched his side, and a blunt arrow dropped to the ground. I looked to the hole in the wall, and there they were: Bri, Hayyan, and Marcus, bows ready, arrows prepped on the ground in front of them.

I ran with everything I had left. My hooves hit the ground so hard I thought they would crack. Bri was too weak to fire anything that would do more than scare them, but every arrow that Marcus fired from his huge bow forced a scream from behind me. Hayyan's smaller bow didn't force the screams that Marcus's did, but just keeping the guards dodging would be enough.

I was getting space. I was going to make it to the hole. Then, in the dark, with Hayyan's traps, we would escape. I just had to keep running.

An arrow hit me in the back of my thigh. I had forgotten about their archer.

My leg burned and shook as my hoof hit the ground, but it didn't give out. I staggered but lumbered forward. I glanced back, and guards hadn't caught me. The arrows had kept them at bay.

I would make it.

Then I yawned. My axe dropped from my hand. I stared at my short brown fingers as they blurred. I tried to blink it away, but I could barely open my eyes again.

"Sleep arrow," I mumbled, not even sure why I was saying it. My thoughts seemed to stretch out, sentences abandoning me.

I needed to sleep.

No. Keep walking. Sleep safehouse. Later. Keep go.

Step. Step.

Step.

Ground hard.

CAPTURE

"Yryja should have killed you," a male voice said. "Guess I'll have to do it for her."

I opened my eyes, but the world was nothing more than a blur of brown, grey, and purple.

"I cannot imagine what would have motivated you to come back, knowing you'd find me here. But I should not expect intelligence from a monster." The voice laughed. It was deep and cruel.

I tried to rise, but I was strapped to whatever I was lying on. And I had no strength to push against it.

"I knew you were nothing but a beast from the moment I saw you."

My whole body shook. I felt tiny and helpless, like a terrified child. I had heard that voice so long ago, smashing up against Jon's cold steel.

"You took Rorvin from me," he said. "You showed me the evil you are. And now everyone will know I can protect them from evil like you."

Valence.

But he wasn't from Castulo. How long had I been out? Had he come to Castulo? Had I been taken away?

Had Bri and Hayyan escaped?

I remembered Bri's haggard form, barely able to fire arrows to cover my escape. If he had tried to save me . . .

For the first time, I understood Delsaran's words on choice. Krek had his talons around my throat, but I would come here again to fight for Bri and Hayyan.

I still wanted to escape, though.

But my breathing slowed, and I relaxed. The world became less blurry; blobs of colour turned into shapes. I could hear Valence handling something behind me, followed by a click of metal on metal.

"Only I can stop those who would wreck Castulo," Valence ranted. "Jon said he brought wealth to the people, but all he did was destroy our way of life."

I gripped my hand into a clumsy fist. I had to fight Valence, somehow. But there was nothing I could do—yet.

"One, three," he said. "Pick up this table and carry it, then follow me." I looked for who he was talking to, then two stone golems came into view, splotches of colour resolving themselves into pink and red corundum eyes. Marcus had said golems attacked him. It had likely been Valence, then. But why would Valence want Jon?

The golems looked past me to the table as they picked it up, registering nothing but what they were told to see. Their heads swiveled where a crack separated their head from their body, stone grinding upon stone.

As they waited for Valence to start walking, I examined the large room. Dark, jagged golems filled it from rune-lined wall to rune-lined wall. The strange-yet-familiar runes travelled up the wall and across the ceiling, then met in a pillar in the middle of the room. The runes were only broken by a staircase that curved along the wall, leading higher into the tower.

The golems lifted the table. I felt myself sway against the straps as they carried me out a large door.

The sun blinded me for a moment, shining straight down into my eyes. I squinted and turned my head as far away as I could. Slowly, my vision came back, and I saw I was still in old Castulo. I had been in the new tower in the centre of the city.

Valence stepped onto to a platform to address the marketplace. "This is the monster that killed my son!" His voice echoed off the distant buildings. "Beasts like this one come from far-off lands and threaten our children. How do they come here? Traitors travel to those lands, claiming that trade will bring us wealth. But what can they bring us that we do not produce ourselves? Only death!"

Heads turned toward Valence as he spoke. "I am the wall that protects you. I will deal with the monsters who seek to destroy you."

I strained against my bonds, stretched my muzzle to bite at them, and even tried to make my hands glow with magic. But my bonds remained tight.

Meanwhile, wealthy citizens in flowing robes and workers in old, patched clothes alike gathered around Valence. I recognised a few, and lists of tastes flashed in memory. Elbert, Huxian whiskey; Reginald, cucumber water; Brigette, kloidale. They looked on with pity—but said nothing. The rest looked on with scorn.

"The wave of evil crashes against me in vain!" Valence continued. "Castulo has fallen from greatness. But you see the evil coming to our land. You see these monsters. And now you see that I will protect you and put this monster to death!"

If I could persuade Elbert, Reginald, and Brigette to help, I had a chance, however slim. I looked them in the eyes and began to speak. "Many of you know me and know my story. I am a threat to no one. Yes, by accident I killed Rorvin—"

"He admits it!" Valence screamed. "He admits he is a murderer who will destroy Castulo!"

"And do you admit what you did to Jon?" I projected my voice through the market. "And what you did to his friends?"

"The monster dissembles to save himself!" Valence laughed.

I focused on those I had to persuade. "You knew Jon. He was always honest. And he wanted the best for Castulo and everyone in it."

"Honest men do not keep murderers as pets," Valence sneered. "They do not feed beasts and grow them into monsters."

"Are you really better off without Jon?" I asked. "I only see more poverty and—"

"One, hold his muzzle shut!" Valence shouted.

The golem reached for my muzzle, and my words turned into a muffled scream as the jagged edges of its hands dug into my flesh.

"The evil that threatens you is weak to me!"

I looked at the few who might help, but they simply stared at me, their lips pursed in silent pity. The rest of the audience shook their fists and cheered.

What else could I do?

"The last year has been hard, but I will make you safe again," Valence said. "I will drive out all who would harm you!"

"Are you killing yourself, then?" The man's voice was cocky, but it rang clear. Though deeper now, I had heard it before, so long ago.

Bri.

Alone, he walked up to the crowd around me. He was still emaciated, but yesterday he had barely been able to draw his bow; today, he looked like he was ready to take on both golems by himself.

His bow was strapped to his back, and a long green cloak fluttered in the wind behind him. He swaggered towards Valence as though he were the hero of all the fantasies we had imagined as children.

"Because the only one who threatens Castulo," he said, his arm shooting out and sending his cape flying, "is you."

Valence's face hardened. "You are a criminal. If not for this beast breaking you out of prison, you would still be there, rotting for your crimes."

Bri slowly unfastened his bow from his back, then placed one end on the ground in front of him. He leaned against it, smiling. "Do you want to tell them what you did to me? What you did to my mother?"

"I punished those who would harm Castulo! Just being friends with this monster proves you are evil." Valence stepped forward, his hand jabbing toward Bri.

Bri was distracting Valence, I realised. Avinna, Marcus, and Hayyan must be nearby. But the golem held my muzzle tight, and I could only look at Bri.

Bri lifted his bow, and everyone in the crowd watched. His voice grew louder as he spoke. "Harm Castulo? By protecting someone who tried to make the world better?" His hand inched into the quiver at his hip, and he began to draw an arrow.

I felt delicate, nimble hands touch my fur and start working on the straps. "Hayyan," I breathed, as they undid one strap after another. Then Avinna grabbed the golem's hand and tried to pry it off my muzzle, but the stony mitt wouldn't budge.

"You threaten me here and claim innocence? You expect anyone to believe you just protected someone while you draw your bow at me? These people are too smart to fall for your tricks!" Valence ranted.

Hayyan finished with the straps and reached for the golem's hand. They pulled at it with Avinna, but the pressure on my muzzle barely lessened.

"If they've been fooled by you, then perhaps not," Bri called out. The intensity in his face and voice was mesmerizing. He nocked his arrow and aimed, as though he could draw and fire at any moment. The crowd was entranced.

"Number one, number three!" Valence shouted. "Stop him!"

The golem released my muzzle and stepped toward Bri.

I rolled off the table, but my legs collapsed beneath me, and I fell to the ground with a thud. Valence turned at the sound and saw us.

"Kill them! Kill them! Kill them! Kill them!" he screamed, pointing at me.

The golems lumbered toward me. I tried to push myself to my knees, but my arms couldn't lift my body, and the golems moved quickly. One raised its hand to strike me. I tried to roll away but didn't have the strength to roll over my arm. The golem swung, and the massive rock of a fist sped towards me.

Then Avinna caught its fist with both hands. Her feet dug into the ground, and she fought against the golem. I finished my roll. Then the golem's strength overwhelmed even Avinna's, and her hands smashed against the rock where I had lain a moment before. A crunch of bone and stone carried across the marketplace.

Two voices screamed at once: "Avinna!" "Mom!" Metal plinked against stone as arrows struck the golems.

I looked over and saw Hayyan's feet as they leaped back over their spear. Their hand darted down and grabbed the spear as the other golem lumbered toward them.

I tried to force myself to my feet and heard another plink, then a crack. "Hayyan, Chase, the eyes!" Bri shouted. "The eyes can be shattered!"

Avinna still stood between me and the golem. One of its eyes had shattered, and bits of ruby littered its torso. But it ignored Avinna and swung at me again, as fast as before.

Avinna blocked the punch with her forearm. I heard another crack, and her arm bent as she screamed. She dropped to one knee, but still faced the golem.

"Come on, you dumb hunk of rock," Avinna grunted. "I'm your enemy."

The golem ignored her. It pulled its arm back to swing again.

But Avinna's good arm speared out at the golem's remaining eye. Her crooked fingers couldn't damage the gem, but the golem didn't know that. It stopped its punch and blocked her arm, knocking it to the side, then swung at Avinna.

Avinna leapt back, and the fist passed just in front of her. Then she hopped back again, and the golem chased her. Its fists swung hard and fast, but Avinna bobbed and weaved around each one.

She glanced beside me; I followed her eyes and saw her sword and shield. She must have dropped them to get me free. I crawled over to them, my legs and arms finally able to support my weight.

Carefully, I picked them up and got to my feet.

I glanced over at Hayyan. They were doing as well as could be expected against the golem. They danced around it, then poked at its eyes, forcing the golem to block.

But Avinna had no weapon to fight back, and she was rapidly running out of space to dodge into. She tried to circle around the golem that chased her, but its blurry fist forced her back again. Another two arrows plinged off its face, narrowly missing its remaining eye.

I tested my legs. Each time I bent my knees, they sprang back faster.

Avinna stepped back against a wall. The golem punched, and Avinna dodged. The fist just missed her, striking the wall and cracking it. Avinna dropped low and tried to sneak between its legs, but another fist smashed into the ground, and I felt the vibrations through the earth.

I charged.

Two more punches, each one narrowly missing Avinna's face. Then the third caught her dark hair, pinning her against the wall. With a yell, she pulled herself free, leaving tufts of hair in the cracks of the wall—but the golem's next punch already careened toward her.

Then I was there. I took the blow on my shield and the screech of wrenched metal filled the market. It knocked me into Avinna and against the wall—only luck kept me on my hooves. My shield had warped, leaving the outline of the golem's fist deep in the metal. My shield could not take many more blows. And I was not the best at dodging.

But better it attacked me than Avinna. I poked at its eye, and it knocked my sword out of the way, then swung at me.

I danced to the side, but not fast enough. It struck my shield with a glancing blow, and I spun in place. The world reeled as it attacked again and struck dead centre on my shield. I flew back, landing on my ass.

It charged. Dropping my sword, I rolled with my momentum and got to my feet just in time to jump back as it swung again—but not far enough. The golem struck another glancing blow against my shield, warping it into a hunk of twisted metal.

Avinna's voice, strained with pain, broke through the haze of battle. "Valence is running into the tower!"

I kept my eyes on the golem in front of me. I couldn't take any chances. Just one of those punches would flatten me.

"We've got Chase—we don't need him," Hayyan shouted back.

"He's got a whole army of golems in there!" I yelled.

Avinna cursed and ran.

I risked a glance at Avinna. Valence was not a good runner, but he had a head start, and Avinna struggled through the pain of her injuries.

Out of the corner of my eye, I saw the golem's attack coming, and leapt to the side. But the golem was still too fast. My shield crumpled around its fist, trapping my hand inside it.

All I could do now was dodge.

It swung again, and I dove. Its hand passed just over me as I landed on my belly.

It pressed forward and stomped down. I rolled, desperate to get out of range; the ground shook as its foot landed next to me.

Before I could stand, its other leg was already up in the air. I rolled again, but I seemed to move in slow motion as the foot sped towards me.

"Chase!" Bri shouted, then his arrow struck home, shattering the second eye of the golem.

Its leg stopped just above my body, then the golem toppled over, landing on me. The golem knocked the breath out of me, but I was alive. I tried to wriggle my way free and looked over while I did so.

Hayyan was still fighting their golem, but they were quicker than me. They slid past each punch, then jabbed at the golem's eyes to keep it defensive. Finally, they leapt forward, stabbing into the golem's eye. I heard the gem shatter, but the golem's other arm broke Hayyan's spear just in front of their hands.

Hayyan stumbled back, but still managed to twirl away from the next punch. They stopped on their toes, ready to spring in any direction. Then Marcus's arrow hit its mark, shattering the other eye, and the golem fell, dead.

I tried to catch my breath before remembering Avinna. I looked at the tower, and saw Valence run through the door. Avinna hadn't been able to catch him.

"Chase, you said there's a whole army of golems in there?" Bri asked.

I nodded, unable to speak with the golem on top of me.

"Mom! We have to go!" Bri shouted.

Avinna turned back to Bri and ran. Her face contorted in pain each time her foot hit the ground. And the ground shook as more than a hundred golems started running at the same time.

Bri, Marcus, and Hayyan lifted the golem off me as Avinna reached us. I got to my feet, grabbed my sword, then the doors flew open, and golems poured out of the tower. They chased after us, fast for their massive size. We ducked down one alley, then another, turning at every house we could, hoping we were fast enough that they wouldn't see us.

Finally, the only sound was our panting breaths, and the ground was still. We caught our breath, and, though wounded and hunted, we smiled at each other, happy. For the first time, my new family was together.

Now I just had to make sure we stayed that way.

SUBTERFUGE

"**B**ri," I whispered. "I can't believe I'm seeing you again."
I held him tight and remembered all those nights I had dreamt of him. Bri's strong arms hugged me back.

We stood in the middle of Marcus's small, poorly lit safehouse. Marcus had set Avinna's bones, and, thankfully, the breaks had been clean. Her broken arm now rested in a sling, and her fingers were bandaged together. They sat on the narrow bed in one corner, and Hayyan sat in the chair in the other.

"I can't believe you're alive," Bri said. "I have so much to tell you about. There's so much I've done!" He laughed like we were children again. "Did you watch me walk through that angry mob and make Valence shake?"

"My heart fluttered when I saw you. You could have taken both of those golems yourself."

Bri's smile faltered for a second. "Those two, yes," he said. He forced his smile back, then opened his mouth to speak but nothing came out.

I cursed myself. "Marcus told me what happened to Jon."

"I fired arrow after arrow as the golems surrounded me. I stood tall to the last."

"Just like you always do."

It was so easy to fall into my old place with Bri. I basked in his glory—both real and imagined. I wanted to follow Bri wherever he led.

But not yet.

"How did Valence get control of Castulo?" I asked.

"After you faked your death," Bri said, "Jon set up an organisation to fight for the worker and the world. Then he left. He said he didn't know his place in the world anymore and he had to find it again." Bri sighed. "Valence came to Castulo to run the organisation. He convinced everyone that he had the most experience holding others to account.

"I knew he was evil after he tried to kill you, but I didn't know how to convince anyone. When Jon said he was coming back, I thought he could help me fix it, but, well . . ."

"You did everything a person could," I said.

Marcus coughed, then spoke. "After Brimark and Avinna were captured, I milked every connection I had, from the Lord Provost to my old adventuring pals. But my connections are not as good as they once were." He grimaced. "Or Valence's were better.

"I never found any trace of Jon. I didn't even know Valence was connected until today. But keeping people in prison, well, that creates a paper trail." Marcus looked at me and Hayyan. "And that's where I met you."

I nodded.

"What do we do next?" Avinna said.

"Valence is behind all this, so we stop him," Bri said. "He's got his army of golems, sure, but they took us by surprise last time. We have all the skill we need to take him out."

My chest tightened. He was braver than I could ever be, but Delsaran had had that kind of courage, and I knew where it led.

"This isn't just our fight," I said before I could think. "Valence has worked his way into the city. It's their responsibility, too."

Bri turned away and stared at the corner of the small room. I felt like I had betrayed him, even though I knew that wasn't true.

There was an awkward pause before Hayyan asked, "Then what do you think we should do, Chase?"

I took a breath. "We need to speak to the Lord Provost. I need to face the people who condemned me to death."

"You can't bring your weapons in here," the guard said. She studied my horns with an idle curiosity that had been crushed by boredom and routine.

Bri held his bow tightly. "Is there any way we can keep them?" he asked. He looked up at the large, carved doors of city hall as though he considered breaking through them. But the doors dwarfed us; I could stand on my shoulders three times and my horns still wouldn't hit the top of the doorway.

"Not if you want to make your way inside," the guard droned. She clearly did not take the idea of Bri fighting his way in seriously.

I imagined bashing through the door and confronting the Lord Provost with my axe. It would not be the best way to convince him that I was, in fact, not a murderer. I took a breath and said, "Talking is our only chance."

Hayyan's spear had been broken, and Avinna's bandaged fingers couldn't hold her weapons, so they were already disarmed. I gave Avinna's sword to the guard, and Marcus gave his bow. Bri grumbled, but eventually handed his bow to her as well, and we walked into the building.

Hayyan stared at the many-arched ceiling, its stone ribs fanning out through etchings of lions wielding hammers and quills—the symbols of Castulo.

"Chase, what's the plan?" Hayyan asked. "It's your life on the line."

"Jon taught me how to argue. But I still freeze under stress."

"Can someone else really argue it for you?" Hayyan said.

I had no answer to that. I tried to remind myself that I had made so much progress, but knew it meant nothing if I couldn't save my own life.

"I can step in if you don't know what to say, Chase." Marcus soothed. "I'm good at oratory."

I nodded, digging my fingers into my leg as we walked into the gallery of the council chamber.

The Lord Provost's white hair clung to the side of his face as he sat at the head of a long, richly varnished, semi-circular table. The rest of the council sat around him, dressed well in silk robes. Stained glass gave everything a golden hue, and my hooves sunk deep into the plush Kashan carpet.

"How do we get their attention?" Hayyan asked.

It was not a question we needed to answer. The Lord Provost spotted me and stared; his large eyes widened until they crowded his thin nose.

"Chase?" the Lord Provost said. "I thought you were dead."

I opened my mouth, and my mind went blank.

"Many times over, my lord," Marcus said. "Most recently by Valence, who attempted to execute him this morning, without your knowledge."

Most of the council stared at me in shock, though several faces I didn't recognise whispered to their neighbours in confused tones.

The Lord Provost climbed to his feet, his hands gripping the table, then said, "I cannot fault Valence for his actions. Chase did kill his son."

"He thought he was saving my life," Bri said, his voice hard.

"From some rough play? Even I am bound by our laws."

Bri's fists clenched. He opened his mouth, but Marcus gripped his bulging forearms. "I know, son," he whispered, "but it will not help."

Hayyan filled the silence. "For as long as I have known Chase, he has done nothing but fight to help those around him. Can you look at Chase and tell me that's right?"

"But Valence, too, has done nothing but work for the well-being of society. He ensures the city grows for the good of all—and the future." He ran his fingers along the table. "And he has not killed anyone."

Marcus motioned for Hayyan to move back. "Valence is not who you think he is, my lord. He captured Jon Galat and imprisoned my wife and son to further his own goals, whatever they are. I guarantee they do not include the good of the city."

The Lord Provost's knuckles turned white. I knew I should say something, but what? There were no laws I could argue, and Marcus knew more about Valence.

"Do you have any proof?" the Lord Provost asked.

"His golems kidnapped Jon. He never forgave Jon for what happened to his son," Marcus said. His eyes stared into the distance. "And," he continued, "Valence has gained a lot of power in Jon's absence."

"How do you know they were Valence's golems?"

"He commanded the same golems this morning when he tried to execute Chase."

"Can you tell one golem from another with such certainty?" The Lord Provost shook his head. "Jon paid for the golems that Valence commands."

"Valence has more golems than you know. And Jon would not have wanted to be kidnapped." Marcus's voice was cold.

"I have the affirmed desires of Jon here, and only your words against them."

The Lord Provost was right: we had no proof. What could I say to convince him?

Remember the first rule of combat, I heard Delsaran say. *v*

I didn't need to convince him Valence was responsible. I just needed to convince him Valence was worth investigating.

"Lord Provost," I projected. "Jon had many talents and a brilliant intellect, but he only ever saw what was right in front of him. So do we all. We are shaped more by the circumstances of our life than our intelligence.

"What happens when harm is spread thinly over thousands while benefits are clumped upon a few? The few clamour, while the thousands scarcely manage to squeak in protest. Thus does evil recommend itself."

I felt myself falling into my rhythm; my voice rose and fell in pitch, and my hands flowed across my body. "Valence may be empowered for the good of Castulo, but when he confronts those who would profit from the harm they inflict, he receives only ire as he rebukes them, and only praise as he caves. Have you provided enough pressure to balance the scales?"

The Lord Provost's face contorted as though he were looking at a hair that just would not stay in place.

"You corner me like Jon used to," he said. Then he sighed. "Very well, I will summon Valence to hear these accusations himself." The Lord Provost nodded toward a guard by the door, and said, "Fetch him." The guard stepped out.

We let out a breath.

Then the Lord Provost looked to his council. "Let us recess until Valence arrives. I have no stomach for figures now."

The council stood and walked out, leaving us alone in the gallery.

I looked back. Avinna's good arm was wrapped around Bri, whose face was flushed.

"You—" Bri said, then twisted his foot in the carpet. "You spoke well." He pushed Avinna's arm away and stood with his back straight. "I am sorry that I did not help."

My heart lurched, and I took his hand. "I still wouldn't be here if you hadn't stood against Valence alone."

He smiled half-heartedly. "Still a hero?"

"Always," I said, holding his hand.

Avinna's hard voice broke the moment. "We need a plan for when Valence gets here."

"Chase," Marcus said, "you know him best. What will he try to do?"

"Jon said he was a narcissist. He only cares about himself and will attack anyone he doesn't see as his equal or superior."

Marcus stroked his chin. "That's good to know. What do we have against him if he tries that?"

"He threw me and Brimark in jail," Avinna said.

"He tried to kill Chase with his golems," Bri said.

"Both awful, yes," Marcus said. "But nothing we haven't already said." Marcus looked down at the empty council table. "It's just word against word. And the status quo is in his favour."

Marcus leaned over the railing of the gallery. "Chase, I don't suppose you have any more clutch speeches to pull out?"

"Not that I can think of. But then, I didn't exactly plan that one."

Marcus stared at me, then turned back to the council chamber. "Then we play the cards we have and pray to Dimione that it's enough."

Hayyan touched me on the shoulder, and whispered into my ear, "Will you be all right if he attacks you?"

"Of course," I responded automatically.

"Good," they said. "Only, I can hear your breathing."

I listened to my own breaths, shallow and fast. I tried to force myself to breathe deep, but my breaths sputtered in my belly.

Then Valence entered the council chamber. His eyes blazed; they sought out mine and bore into me as he walked up to the table facing the Lord Provost's seat.

A guard entered the gallery. He ushered us through hallways lined with tapestries and into the main chamber, then to a table beside Valence. He looked at me as though he were a lion ready to pounce.

The doors at the back of the room opened and the Lord Provost stepped through, followed by the other members of the council.

Valence bowed deep as they took their seats. We quickly followed suit.

"The Right Honourable Lord Provost, it is always such a pleasure to be in your presence," Valence said. "Simply seeing your face inspires me to be better, and your wisdom is forever a guiding force in my life."

Hayyan quietly snorted with disgust.

"Valence," said the Lord Provost, "these people claim that you tried to execute Chase without our authority, you imprisoned some of them without cause, and you kidnapped Jon Galat." He turned to us. "Did I represent your claims fairly?"

Marcus stood as straight and still as I had ever seen him. "Those are our claims, Lord Provost."

The Lord Provost looked over at Valence. "Do you have any response to these claims?"

Valence bowed again, his chest almost touching the floor. "My Lord Provost," he said, "I admit that upon seeing Chase, I lost my head. Under normal circumstances, I would never do anything that you had not authorized. But you know how I mourn the loss of my son."

The Lord Provost nodded.

Then Valence continued. "And these miscreants likely failed to mention that Chase orchestrated the attack on the prison last night, demonstrating the depths of his pugnacious nature and depravity."

"Is this true, Chase?" the Lord Provost asked. While he spoke, Valence met my eyes and grinned with unbridled glee. But the smile disappeared before anyone else could see.

"It is true in part," Marcus responded. "My wife and son were imprisoned there. All my efforts to discover the reason for their imprisonment were blocked—for reasons I now understand," he said, looking at Valence.

"So, you hired a known murderer to help you break the law?" Valence asked. "And you expect us to believe that you're telling the truth?"

"Chase is a friend," Marcus said, his voice controlled but his jaw stiff. "He helped because he has known Brimark, my son, for years."

"And you think being friends with a murderer is a point in your defence?"

My chest tightened. I had been ready for Valence to attack me. I had been ready to be apprehended and thought it a fair price to save Bri. But I had not been ready for Valence to use me to attack them.

Marcus ignored Valence and spoke to the Lord Provost directly. "I have to ask, has Valence made life in Castulo better?"

Valence shouted, "Everything I've done has been for the good of Castulo!"

But Marcus's voice commanded attention. "I have watched the slums grow and villages falter. Factories lay vacant while poorhouses bustle."

"These are all lies."

"For the good of Castulo?" Marcus scoffed. "The only good he can conceive of is his own."

"I alone make decisions for the good of Castulo, while you fight like any one of a thousand sellswords. You are nothing but a leech."

This was degrading into mudslinging. The Lord Provost hands' pressed against the table, and he prepared to stand. If he cut us off, Valence won. My mind raced, trying to think of something to say.

Valence thought that his position—his money, his power, his skills—made him more important than anyone else. A fool, according to Jon. A self-important bureaucrat, according to Delsaran.

A monster, according to me. I stamped down the anger that welled up in me. *Rewards from obedience—*

No. I was not that small child. I would not be that small child again.

I seized my anger and burned away my fears. But I did not let my anger overtake me. I knew just how to make Valence break, so long as I could keep my head. I didn't have to show the Lord Provost who I was. I just had to show the Lord Provost who Valence was.

"Valence understands nothing of society." My voice boomed. "He has skills and talents that others lack, I grant you that. And he should be encouraged to use them. But society survives because we better it as we better ourselves; when chained by misfortune, our thrashing must break the bonds of those around us. Society exists for all its members, or soon it will not exist at all.

"Without miners swinging in the fetid dark, without farmers planting under the burning sun, and without clerks smiling into vicious abuse, he would have no decisions to make. Alone, he would forage to survive, or he would die."

Valence glowered at me. "They all depend on me! You are nothing but a jealous, murderous leech who cannot stand the thought of someone better than you. Nothing you say can change you from the monster you are!"

"They depend upon you? Is that what you say to the people you steal from? It seems to me that you've done quite well for yourself. But Jon built his wealth from nothing; you take the wealth that others have made."

Valence's face was red, his chest rigid. "You dare insult me? You who murdered my son!"

The Lord Provost opened his mouth to interject. I needed to break Valence now.

"Could you really kill anyone?" I asked.

"I killed Jon and I can kill you!"

The air rushed out of me. I stepped back, my hoof landing hard on the carpet.

"That's right, little cow," Valence said. "You are nothing to me and will soon be even less."

"Valence!" The Lord Provost shouted. Valence jumped and then slowly turned to face the Lord Provost.

"Yes, my Lord Provost," Valence snivelled.

"I trusted you and your words. I can't believe . . ." The Lord Provost stared at Valence. "Well, you said it. I will have to ask you to stand trial."

Valence sliced through the air with his hand. "Don't you dare think you're better than me. I am the only one who has ever cared about Castulo."

The Lord Provost motioned to the guards, and they moved toward Valence.

Valence laughed. "After this morning, did you not think I would come prepared?"

He lifted his wrist to his mouth, and said, "All numbers, to me!" His voice boomed out unnaturally loud, and the stone walls shook. I covered my ears, but my hands did nothing to soften their agony.

The Lord Provost opened his mouth and spoke, but I heard only ringing.

Valence grinned.

The Lord Provost spoke again, and I could just make out the words. "What did you do?"

"His golems!" Hayyan shouted as though far away.

They burst through the door, the wood splintering. An endless stream of them entered the chamber, shoulder to shoulder.

Valence cackled. "You will all pay for this. Your lives will feed my future!" The golems surrounded him, blocking him from view. "All numbers, take me to my tower!"

Valence laughed the whole way out as we stood there, stunned.

After he left, Avinna was the first to speak. "What did he mean by that? Our lives will feed his future?"

What did he have in his tower besides the golems? I could only think of those strange-yet-familiar runes that covered the ceiling, pillar, and walls. They had unnerved me then, but—

"Nightbringers," I whispered. "He's going to turn us all into nightbringers."

V

RECONNAISSANCE

"Nightbringers, again," Hayyan whispered. "They've taken over my whole life."

Bri put his hand on Hayyan's shoulder. "We'll deal with them, don't worry."

"What are they?" Marcus asked.

"Creatures of magic," Hayyan said, their voice flat. "Essentially mindless. They just search out life and kill it."

"At least they were when we fought them," I said. "Those . . . did not go according to plan."

Hayyan tilted their head, but before I could elaborate, Marcus asked another question: "How did they end up here?"

"I brought a mage to look at the Nightbringers. He said he would send information to a colleague here, but I didn't think anything of it at the time."

"We can't fault you for that, Chase," Hayyan said.

"How do we fight them?" Avinna asked.

"Arrows and piercing weapons will slow them, but you need to cut off a piece to kill them." I shook my head. "But that's not the real threat."

"What do you mean?" asked Hayyan.

"Creating the nightbringers drained the life out of everything within sight, from the plants to the people. And Valence's tower is much bigger than the room near Greenchapel."

"Meaning he could take out the whole city," Marcus said.

I nodded.

"How do you know this, Chase?" the Lord Provost asked. I had forgotten he was in the chamber with us.

"When I was gone, my Lord Provost, Delsaran took me to a town under attack by them. We tracked down the source of them, but Delsaran"—I swallowed the lump in my throat—"fell in the battle."

The council members chittered to each other while the Lord Provost collapsed into his seat. The council members babbled at him, but he just murmured, "Valence. Why?"

"We know how they're made," Avinna said. "And how to kill them. But how do we stop Valence?"

I looked over at Marcus, but he just looked back at me, and said, "Part of being a leader is knowing when to step back and let someone else take over. You're the one with experience fighting these"—he paused to make sure he got the word right—"nightbringers."

"You're the only one who's seen how they were made," Hayyan said.

My hands shook. It had been hard enough to speak up for myself; how could I lead a city?

I looked at Bri for guidance. I had always followed him before. But Bri scowled at me. "Do it, Chase," he said. "They're right. You're the only one who can."

"What do we need?" Marcus asked.

I stared at Bri, unable to think of anything but his scowl.

"Tell them what they need to know, Chase," Bri growled.

Bri was right. If we didn't fix this, neither of us would be alive. I could deal with Bri's anger later. I took a breath and tried to clear my head. "We have to destroy the crystal," I said. "But it's tough. Delsaran attacked it with all his magic but only cracked it."

Everyone looked at me, but I had nothing more to say. I dug my fingers into my leg.

Marcus looked at the Lord Provost. "Do you have any blasting clay?"

"I believe we use it for demolition and defense."

"Chase, would that work?"

I had no way of knowing if it would work. Was there anyone who would? "The mage Valence worked with on his tower might know."

"He used to work in the city," the Lord Provost said, "but I haven't seen him since he finished Valence's tower. Valence said he left."

"Valence said the same thing about Jon," Avinna said.

I sighed. It was time to do what needed doing. "Let's go with the blasting clay unless we think of a better idea. Where do we get it?"

The Lord Provost motioned to a guard standing by the semicircular table, then said, "Take them to the armory and get them whatever they need."

"Thank you," I said.

I strode after the guard but was interrupted by Marcus. "Then there are the golems."

"Right," I said. I remembered Marcus's own words. "But you have more experience with those."

Marcus nodded. "He'll likely use the golems to protect the tower." He turned to the Lord Provost. "Do your troops have experience fighting golems?"

"The city guard doesn't see much actual combat" he replied. "It mostly just keeps the peace."

"That sounds like my job, then," Marcus said. "I can lead the battle against them."

"I fought against them too," Bri said. "And I'm just as good an archer as you are."

His words were a weight on my chest. Was this what he was angry about? Did he feel useless? "I can only survive if you slow the night-bringers with your arrows. And my axe can't do much against the golems' eyes. I need you, Bri."

"Leave that to me," he said. "You'll be my shield, Chase." He smiled, though his eyes were still narrow.

"And I always will be," I whispered so quiet that he didn't hear me.

The weight on my chest lifted, I thought about what else needed to be done. "Hayyan," I said, "Valence probably activated the crystal on a small scale before. You're the only other one who has experience fighting nightbringers, so I'll need you."

They nodded, their feet shifting on the soft carpet.

"Anything I can do?" Avinna asked, holding up her bandaged hand.

Against nightbringers and golems, she wouldn't be able to fight. But that wasn't all that needed doing. "We need to get people to safety in case we can't stop this. They're going to be scared, confused, and in denial. And no one can knock sense into people like you, Avinna."

She smiled. "If they try to ignore me, I've still got my legs to boot them to safety."

Her smile felt good. And only then did I realise I had taken charge. I had thought that a leader commanded like a general on a battlefield, barking orders to those beneath them.

I could never do that. I wanted too much to make everyone happy. But I could still lead in my own way by finding what everyone did well and exciting them for it.

"All right," I said to the Lord Provost. "You have any issues with the plan?"

"No," he said. "My guard here will be able to lead you to the armoury. Good luck."

"If you're leaving, let's go together," Avinna said, walking up to the Lord Provost. They were even in height, but she towered over him. "You can put the weight of your office behind my words."

The Lord Provost nodded, hiding a frown.

Marcus reached out and touched Avinna's cheek. "Good luck, my love," he said.

She nodded back at him with a smile. "And to you, love." Then she looked at Bri. "I know you'll make me proud."

Her goodbyes complete, she walked to the doors, leaving the Lord Provost to follow her.

"Before you leave," Marcus called after the Lord Provost, "where's your city guard now?"

The Lord Provost's mouth hung open. Then the guard said, "Anyone who realises something is happening will meet at the guardhouse. It's next to the armory, and that's where I'm taking those three," he said, motioning to me, Bri, and Hayyan.

Marcus nodded. "We'll head there together."

Avinna walked out the door, the Lord Provost struggling to keep up with her.

I watched Avinna go, then looked at Hayyan and Bri. I had lost so much in my life. But they cared for me and, what's more, respected me. Every time I spoke, I still feared I'd be ignored—or worse. But now my family was ready to march on my plan.

And we had a city to save.

Broken posts and signs lined the street, and the setts had cracked beneath the golems' weight. For a while, we could hear Avinna shouting as she evacuated people, but soon that faded, and the city was silent.

We rushed through empty streets to the armoury and guardhouse. They were large, squat buildings, expanded over generations. Between each floor, the brick changed colour slightly, red on the bottom floor, rust on the second, and pink on the third.

The guard walked up to the armory and spoke to two sentries lounging outside. Word hadn't reached them yet, and they didn't believe what they heard until some off-duty guards made their way there and confirmed it.

Then the guard walked back to Marcus. "Let's head into the guardhouse. I'll introduce you to everyone who's here," he said.

Marcus nodded. Then he embraced Bri. "I love you so much, my son. You're everything to me. So come home safe."

"I will, dad," Bri said.

Marcus broke the hug then turned back to the guard. "All right, let's go," he said. They walked into the guardhouse.

Bri watched him go then looked at me and Hayyan and said, "We better head in ourselves." He led the way to the armoury.

"Never met a minotaur before," one sentry said in a gruff voice as we approached the door. Though she didn't seem that curious about me, as she quickly followed it up by asking, "Whad'ya need?"

"Blasting clay," I said. Then I forced myself to add, "And I'll need an axe, shield, and armour."

"Right-o," the sentry said. She opened the door and took us inside the armoury.

The first floor was one big room, divided by shelves filled with almost everything a city guard would need—bows, swords, plate, mail, stirrups, saddles and more.

"Axes are over there, against the wall," she said, pointing to our right. "If ya want plate, it's straight ahead; mail is on its left." Then she motioned to the left. "That's where you'll find the shields." Finally, she waved her hands at the stairs by the door. "Blasting clay, you'll find on the second floor, by the workshops. Third floor's got the offices, but you won't need to see the pencil-pushers."

I walked over to the axes. Behind me, I heard Bri ask about arrows, but I couldn't hear the response over the beating of my heart. My last axe had been made for me by Delsaran. Taking a new one felt like a betrayal.

I breathed, then set the grief and betrayal aside. But even that felt wrong—Delsaran wouldn't have set his emotions aside. He would have revelled in them, and somehow used them to embrace the world. That was his magic.

But I could only stuff my emotions down like Jon.

I grabbed the axe in front of me. I let my emotions churn and imagined myself walking away from them, their voices fading.

Bri returned from gathering arrows as I gave the axe a few practice swings. "Axes suit you, Chase. You look like you could hack through an army by yourself," he said.

"A minotaur's got to have an axe," I said. His words would have touched me like a long-lost lover, but my emotions were already out of earshot.

"You'll want a panga," Hayyan said to Bri. "Or something similar. In case the Nightbringers get close."

"I would look dashing with one on my hip, wouldn't I?" Bri asked.

Hayyan smiled. "You would."

I thanked Hayyan silently and picked out a shield and armour while Bri spent time swinging the machetes, finding one with good balance and an ornate hilt.

I looked through the armour, and remembered the molten metal surrounding Delsaran's burnt flesh.

My heart pounded, and I wanted to run. Take Bri, Hayyan, Marcus, and Avinna—and escape Castulo.

Back in Greenchapel, I had wanted to save my family. When I had returned to Castulo and found Bri missing, I had fought to save him. And then fought to save myself.

But the people of Castulo had accepted my enslavement. Why should I risk my life for them?

I hoped as many got away as possible. But that didn't mean I had to fight for them. Delsaran always did what needed doing—but that answer left my limbs stiff as I grabbed as much blasting clay as I could. All of us could die here—me, Bri, Hayyan, and even Marcus and Avinna.

But if I fled, Bri and Hayyan would fight without me, and I would be alone once more. I couldn't handle that.

I knew I had grown. I had crafted a plan and convinced others to follow it, but so much of who I am was still wrapped up in them. I was still weak. I would fight because they did.

As I left the armory, my stomach was still tight. I hadn't eaten all morning, yet I was not hungry. But my answer loosened my limbs, and I readied myself to swing my axe once more.

I could only hope it would be enough.

ATTACK

Marcus's voice rang clear over the heads and murmurs of the city guard. "Valence has a horde of golems protecting his tower," he said, his voice carrying to us in the back. "If we can defeat him there, we save the city. But we'll need to pull golems away from the tower to do it.

"So, first, we must attack one of the four gates of inner Castulo. If we convince Valence our goal is to break through and evacuate the city, he'll reinforce the gate with golems from the tower. That's when we strike.

"We succeed, or we die. But not just us. My son and wife are here, counting on me. Your family and friends are here, counting on you. Even if they live outside the walls, only you can let them know they must escape. Only you can stop Valence from turning them into monsters.

"Dimione will bless us today. But even if she doesn't, we're going to be Krek-cursed heroes."

A cheer went up from the guards. Bri shouted beside me, and Hayyan followed suit.

It was a short speech—there hadn't been time to prepare a longer one. But this wasn't an order of knights, dreaming of glory. Nor even an army who signed up to fight. This was a throng of people, old and young, with homes, friends, and families. That's who the speech worked for.

I looked at Bri and Hayyan.

And it worked for me.

A couple dozen guards stood ready to cover our assault of the tower. That was all the city could gather on such short notice—Castulo had been safe for a long time. We had avoided the main roads as we approached Valence's tower, then ducked behind the last building before the marketplace.

Now, we waited. I studied the guards, their grey hair, pimply faces, and soft bellies. It would have to be enough.

The dull roar of stone and steel echoed around us. The battle at the walls had begun. My mouth was dry and sandy; I hoped that was from the dust of broken golems.

The mage who came with us tapped me on the shoulder and motioned around the corner. "You probably can't see it," she said, "but a golem's eyes shift when Valence is looking through it."

I examined the golems. They blocked the door in four lines of ten. I looked at the different hues and radiances of their eyes, trying to find out which one denoted intelligence—but how can you know what's different about a gem you've never seen before?

"Not all the golems can be taken over so," the mage said. "We blind the golems Valence sees through, and we blind him."

I nodded, taking another look before ducking back behind the wall. Our plan relied on him not knowing I was here.

I glanced at Bri, who checked his bow and arrows, nocking one, then another, aiming at an imaginary target. When he had gone through all his arrows, he gave a few pointers to some guards who hadn't maintained their training, and they practiced together.

The mage walked away as Hayyan approached. They sat down next to me, their back against the wall.

"How are you feeling, Chase?" they asked.

I debated for a moment, then decided to be honest. "Anxious. Before Valence blocked the gates, part of me just wanted to run away."

They chuckled. "I didn't even think of that as an option until you said it."

The sounds of battle rose, and Hayyan looked toward the walls even though all they could see was the building in front of them. "Ever since I was a child," Hayyan continued, "I've been expected to fight in whatever way I could. Sure, children were given safer jobs, but we still fought.

"Now I'm in the wide world, and I feel the same way. I've had a chance to see so much, but everywhere we go, people are suffering. I just want to do what I can."

I nodded. "Since I was a child, I've been told to forget about what I want. 'There are rewards from obedience, but none from the whip,' I was told. And I believed it.

"I even thought of Delsaran as a kinder, loving owner. He believed in his way of life, so I tried to as well. Only after he"—my throat closed around the word, and I had to choke it out—"died did I realise he wanted me to find my own way.

"Now people look to me for answers. And I'm trying so hard to take charge. But I just wish Bri could lead, or Delsaran or Jon would tell me what to do."

We listened to the distant crash of stone against stone.

"Chase," Hayyan said, "no one masters life. When you think you have it figured out, you have only a half-formed solution to last year's problem. My mom always said, 'It's not about knowing who you are, but about loving who you become.'

"And I've become better because of you, Chase. I couldn't have this conversation before I left Greenchapel."

Bri squatted down in front of me. I hadn't noticed him approaching. "You know, you're not very good at being quiet," he said.

"Sorry, I didn't mean to leave you out. It's just . . . I know this is what you've always wanted. To be a hero. And I'm happy to be your shield, but—"

"You're not my shield," Bri said, his voice hard. "You're the hero."

I froze.

"You're the one who figured out what Valence was up to. You're the one who's fought these nightbringers before. You're the one with the plan. I—I'm the sidekick."

He looked at the brown building opposite us, studying its small windows, then looked back at me with a somber smile. "That's why I was so angry in the council chamber. All this time, I've dreamed of being the hero, with you as my sidekick. You always followed me around, cheering for everything I did. Then, after training for years to become a hero, you suddenly show up and take charge. I'm left doing what you say.

"I know, it's dumb. We have a mission, and a hero shouldn't need their emotions coddled like I did. Krek, you even came back for me. I should be happy. And I am. I missed you, Chase." He grunted. "It just . . . hurt."

"I'm sorry." It was all I could say. I felt like I was breaking apart the little family that I had come all this way to build.

"You have nothing to apologise for," he said, his voice hard. "I'm not the hero I dreamed of today, but Castulo still depends on my bow. I'll fight, and I'll fight well. But, today, it all comes down to you, Chase."

My head spun. Coming here, I had simply wanted to build my own life. But everything I did changed the world around me. It was just like Jon had said, so long ago: our decisions ripple out into infinity. Now I realised it was true of all life.

I couldn't just build my own life; I had to build the world I lived in, too.

Bri punched me in the shoulder. "Just don't think I'm gonna let you take charge next time we save a city, all right?"

I laughed, even as my breath caught. Next time.

I wanted to tell him that I was doing this for him, but let it pass. I couldn't tell him that. Not yet.

But I needed to say one thing: "When the battle comes, you need to take charge. When the pressure's on, I think too much about what the right thing to do is and can't make a decision. I freeze."

Bri studied me, his eyes meeting mine. "I can do that," he said. "But if things go sideways, I'll be depending on your knowledge."

I opened my mouth to speak, but a loud crunch silenced me. More followed. Bri flattened himself against the wall, and the rest of the guard did the same. A few seconds later, a battalion of golems ran down the street, the road cracking beneath them. I counted twenty before they blended into distance and dust. Not as many gone as I had hoped, but it would have to be enough.

We let a few minutes pass in stony silence while I set my doubt and introspection aside.

Finally, the mage peeked around the corner, and said, "Two lines left. More than we can beat, but if we can force a hole through the middle, you'll be able to get in. Hopefully, Valence won't realise you've gone inside, and we can disengage. If not," she said, gazing at me with wide, pleading eyes, "be fast."

She balled her hand by her side. "I'll start off with some lightning. Hopefully, that'll disrupt some of the magic controlling them, and they won't react until it's too late."

She started mumbling words to herself, her fingers grasping at invisible threads. Her hand movements lacked the deft brilliance of Leidre's mage, but the spell went off, lightning crackling along her fist. Then she turned the corner, and the lightning arced out.

I readied my axe and ran.

One of the two golems in front of the door was slumped, its arms and head hanging down. But the other golems swiveled their heads toward us. None seemed to focus on me specifically—hopefully, Valence was focused on the battle at the gate.

The golems stood their ground, two lines of heavy stone. I charged straight for the door, not sure how I was going to get past them.

Then a lightning bolt arced over my shoulder, striking the second golem in front of the door. Its head and arms drooped. I had a path to the door and the other golems didn't know enough to cover their hole. I glanced over the line of guards on either side of me. Hopefully, they would keep the golems' line flat so I could run right through the middle.

We had a chance.

The golems on either side of the stunned ones wouldn't make it easy, though. They raised their stone fists, ready to crush me.

"Chase, can you hold them?" Bri asked.

"I can!" I shouted back.

"Hayyan, go for the door between their legs. I'll cover Chase with my arrows."

Then we were upon them.

I stopped just short of the golem's first strike; the wind from its fist blew over me as Hayyan darted between the legs of the stunned golem. But the golems in the second line weren't looking at me; they were looking at Hayyan.

A few arrows clattered off the golems' faces, but, unperturbed, they swung their heavy fists at Hayyan. Hayyan scrambled back beneath the stunned golem, and the fists hit its stone body; it crashed to the ground and left Hayyan exposed.

They jabbed their spear at the golem on the left, but it knocked their spear aside. The golems pulled back their fists to swing again, but I jumped on top of the fallen golem and jabbed the toe of my axe into the left golem's face.

My axe slipped through and hit the golem's eye. The ruby shattered, red flakes dripping to the ground. I lowed. Then the golems looked at me and swung. Their blows struck my shield at the same time.

My shield crashed into my torso and knocked me off my feet. I hit the ground and slid, the world blurring. My shield hand felt numb.

While the golem attacked me, Hayyan slipped under the second stunned golem and approached the door. They jammed their spear into the lock with a loud clang. But this drew the attention of two golems, whose heads swiveled as Hayyan tried to work the lock. Then the golems swung.

Hayyan dived, leaving their spear in the jamb of the door as their chest hit the ground. They tried to get up, but the golems stomped. Hayyan rolled. The giant feet cracked the ground beside Hayyan.

Then Bri's arrow struck the golem I had hit in its other eye, and it collapsed.

"Nice shot!" I shouted, unsure if Bri could hear me. I got to my feet, discarding the warped shield and gripping my axe in both hands.

Hayyan faced the back row's remaining golem, but without their spear, all they could do was dance around the blows. They dodged with more speed and grace than I ever could, but I knew how exhausting it was to survive against the golems for long.

Only one golem from the front row faced me now—the guards had locked the other golems down. But how long could they hold out? The guards had already taken injuries; some limped back and others lay on the ground, moaning—or silent.

I tried to hatch a plan to take out the golem. If I dove under its fist, I would be too slow to recover. If I kept my distance, Bri would take it out eventually, but would Hayyan and the guards survive until then?

I watched a fist brush against Hayyan's face, sending their hair flying back behind them.

I held my axe in my right hand, then charged. Just as the golem swung at me, I dodged to the right and twisted sideways. I wasn't fast enough to avoid the blow—but I hadn't expected to be.

I reached out as far as I could with my right hand while its fist turned to crush me. I felt the toe of my axe strike the golem's eye as its fist smashed into my ribs. I spun, trying to dissipate the force of the blow, but pain bloomed through my body.

I tasted dirt in my mouth and realised I had fallen. I couldn't remember what was happening; I just knew I had to keep moving.

I struggled to roll over. My arms and legs felt like they bent from the pressure of my weight. I finally managed to roll onto my back and saw the giant grey golem above me. Its fist swung down, and I tried to keep rolling, but my hand slipped along the ground.

Then the arrow struck the golem in its remaining eye, and its fist stopped inches from my chest.

"The hero's supposed to save the sidekick's life at the last second, not the other way around!" Bri shouted.

I climbed to my knees and breathed. My chest hurt, but I didn't think anything was broken; though the golem had struck much harder than any person could, it was a glancing blow, and the armour spread it over my ribs. Still, with each breath, my chest twitched in pain.

I glanced to the side; a couple other golems had been felled by the guards, but many more guards lay sprawled in the dirt. We had a minute at best before the rest of the golems finished with them and turned to us.

I put one hoof down and pushed myself up.

Bri must have had the same thought. He ran past me, his bow strapped over his chest and his panga in hand. Another golem from the back row stepped forward to intercept him, and Bri darted into its range. The golem swung, and Bri leapt to the side. He wasn't as fast as Hayyan, but his panga was better up close.

He tucked himself against the golem's chest, his panga darting up into the golem's eye. The golem blocked it and swung down, but its own bulky body got in the way of its arms.

"Chase!" Bri shouted. "Distract this one for me and I'll break it!"

My ribs ached with each heavy step as I ran over to Bri and poked my axe at the golem's eye. I was too far away to hit it, but the golem didn't know that. The golem swatted my axe away and swung at me. I leapt back as Bri emerged from his spot against the golem's chest, and his panga flashed into the golem's eye.

The gem cracked, and the golem forgot about me. It swung at Bri, forcing him to duck between the golem's legs. It lifted one leg to stomp him, and Bri dove out from under it, sprawling onto the ground. He tried to roll, but his bow was still strapped to his back.

He wriggled from side to side but remained under the golem's rising foot.

As the golem bent down to deliver its final blow, I stepped forward and shoved the toe of my axe right into its eye. It fell over, dead.

"Krek, I've missed you, Chase," Bri said. Then he threw his bow against the door as he shouted to Hayyan, "We'll take this golem; you get the door!"

Hayyan's chest heaved, their breath coming in gasps. The golem lifted its arm, and I stepped forward and poked at its eye.

The golem blocked my axe and attacked me, its fist coming down hard. I dove to the side and heard the crack as its fist hit the ground. Then I landed, and pain stabbed into my bruised ribs.

I worked myself to my feet. The golem took a step forward to hit me again, but Bri was there. Sliding into its range, he thrust his panga into its eye, and the pink gem shattered. But Bri wasn't pressed against the golem's chest this time.

It swung; Bri tried to dodge around its fist, but the golem struck a glancing blow and knocked Bri to the ground. He tried to get up, but the golem pressed him. Bri rolled out of the way of fist after fist, each one smashing the ground closer to his head. Then Bri hit the wall of the tower and stopped. The golem pulled back its fist to swing again. What could I do? I could barely walk, let alone run around the golem to attack its eye.

In desperation, I found the little crack in its knee where stone slid against stone. I gripped my axe with both hands, then swung with all my might.

Sparks flew off my axe as it grinded into the crack, the gravelly screech deafening me. The golem's fist still flew toward Bri, but its leg buckled beneath it. The golem fell back as it completed its punch. It struck the wall, the tower shook, and the golem hit the ground. The haft of my axe snapped as the blade wedged in its knee.

The golem still groped for Bri, but it couldn't reach him.

"That better, sidekick?" I asked Bri between panting breaths. He shot me a glare.

"The door's open!" Hayyan shouted. "Let's go!" Hayyan waved at us with their spear, holding Bri's bow in their other hand.

It was time to stop Valence.

FAILURE

Light pulsed along the runes like a heartbeat. It flowed up the walls and across the ceiling before pooling in the central support pillar, which pumped it through the ceiling with each pulse.

"I guess we go up?" I said. I was not good at this. But I didn't have time to worry about that now. I had to focus on more pressing matters, like my lost axe and shield. If I were lucky, Valence wouldn't have removed them from the room. It had only been this morning, after all. So much had happened in one day.

The room was spacious without the golems. An open floorplan, about 30 paces in diameter, empty now.

I wondered if Marcus had managed to breach a gate, and let people escape. I had no way of knowing, of course. But it would be a relief to know that some people would still escape if I failed.

Either way, I needed my axe and shield. Thankfully, I found them lying on the floor. I bent over them, careful of my bruised ribs. My fingers curled around their grips like a lover's hand.

"Hayyan, Chase," Bri said. "Either of you injured?"

Hayyan looked at the runes lining the walls and ceiling, watching them pulse. "Was it like this last time, Chase?" they asked.

"I'm all right, Bri, just some bruised ribs. And the pulsing light is new, Hayyan."

"Hm?" Hayyan murmured, then realised they hadn't answered Bri's question. "A few cuts and bruises for me, but nothing serious."

"Well, then," Bri said. "Let's do this." I made sure the blasting clay was still safely stowed, and we climbed up the stairs.

The second and third floors of the tower were opulent. Couches filled both rooms, each with deep plush fabric and diamonds embedded in every corner. Tables lay in front of them, surfaced with gems large enough that the tables looked cobblestoned. They made Jon's estate look unadorned and practical.

But as we continued climbing, the rooms looked more and more like storage. Toys, faded paintings of long-dead relatives, ripped and stained clothing, and newspapers with stories about Valence all found their way here, piled haphazardly.

Each floor, the pillar cast the objects in more purple light. As we climbed, the pillar almost overpowered the setting sun streaming in through the large windows on every floor of the tower.

Finally, we reached the top, and my breath caught.

Save for the windows, the walls and ceiling were bare, but in the middle of the room, the central pillar ended in a plinth at chest height, a black crystal like the one I had seen with Delsaran upon it. The pulsing purple light from the pillar fed into the crystal, and it throbbed dully.

Valence was there, but in some kind of glass chamber. Goggles with black lenses covered his eyes, and many seemingly identical pairs sat on a ledge around him. He had a wicked smile on his face, as though he were watching people he hated suffer.

Nightbringers filled the room. I braced to fight them, but they paid us no mind; they just stood there, unmoving. They seemed better-formed than the ones I had known. Each had two arms and two legs that came out at shoulders and hips. But they were angular and long-limbed like all the others.

I felt the wood of my axe bite into my hand.

We crept up the last few stairs, then Valence removed his goggles. He reached down for another pair, but as he lifted the goggles to his face, he saw us. His eyes opened as wide as his mouth, then he recovered. He grinned, picked up a different pair of goggles, and put them on.

He opened his mouth as though he were speaking, but no sound came out—until a second later, when his voice echoed hollowly from the golem on the other end of the room.

"I expected you to flee, monster." He laughed, the sound empty of life. "I would have. I guess that's why I'm smarter than you. Smarter than everyone."

I looked at the crystal in the centre of the room. If I ran, I might be able to make it. But then I'd be surrounded by the nightbringers.

"You killed Rorvin—*my* son," he said. He played with some sort of small wand. It was no more than half a foot long, with a small button on the side. "And now you try to take Castulo from me, too, telling that fool of a provost I am corrupt. I had taken no more than my fair due, running things as I did. I deserve my reward."

Fear froze my limbs. I tried to move or say something, but my body remained still. I had tried to suppress my feelings for so long—the fear, grief, anger, and longing. Just get through the moment, I had always told myself, and deal with them all later. But that was no longer an option. My emotions raged inside me, and I lost myself in them. My mind was a cacophony of voices, and I would have closed my ears to them all if I could. But through the chaos of sound, I chose one voice, and let it be mine.

"Yes, I killed him. He took after you, thinking of other people as his playthings." I used every rhetorical trick I knew for my voice. "You want to know why you're up here in this tower, alone?" I asked, inching toward him—and the crystal. "Because, eventually, people see that beneath your snivelling mask there lies nothing but entitlement and rage."

Valence's lips curled. He tried to smooth his face and seem aloof, but he knew I had seen it.

"You can't imagine the future I have in store for you," he said. "This is a secret I learned from way out west, near Narasi."

"I've fought through your golems twice," I said. "Whatever this secret is, I'll fight through it too."

I repressed a shudder as I crept by the nightbringers. The heat radiated off them. But I had to keep my focus on Valence.

"You'll see how wrong you are soon enough. Or at least your life force will. You'll be one of these creatures. And then you can join your precious Jon again. His life force gave me many of them." He laughed.

My body went limp. "You turned him into a nightbringer?"

"So, you've heard of them before! And probably thought you could distract me with words the way your friend did earlier?"

I looked at the nightbringers around me. Everything I felt about Jon, the anger, the love, and the fear, tightened into a knot that tied me to the ground.

"At least now he'll be useful for something," Valence crooned.

My body quivered. My breath, hot and heavy, curled out of my nostrils. I wanted to launch myself into Valence, axe flashing and shield high. But my limbs remained still.

Bri's arrow shot through the air and struck Valence's chamber. It bounced off the glass and clattered to the ground, knocking me out of my trance.

Valence glared at Bri. "Did you think this would be fragile enough to be broken by one of your arrows?"

I ran for the crystal.

Valence pressed the button on the wand, and a thin light shone from it, striking my chest. Slowly, the nightbringer's arms reached toward me. Valence then aimed the light at Bri and Hayyan, a point of red in the middle of their chests.

The nightbringers charged, a blur of black and red, faster than ever before.

Three on my left, four on my right. I swung my axe through the four on the right, but they were faster. Their black and red hands struck my axe arm, burning me as I cut into them. But my axe still left them as dust.

Then the three on the left reached around my shield, finding my armour. The metal seared my skin and turned my fur to ash. I shrieked but held my ground. We either broke the crystal here, or Valence turned us into nightbringers.

I swung my axe to the left, hacking through the nightbringers there.

I twisted my axe to cleave through the next group, but three nightbringers were already there, reaching for my exposed side. My axe careened toward them, but their hands were only inches from my flesh.

A flash of brown, orange, and silver, and they disintegrated. Hayyan's spear shone in the sunlight as it sliced through them.

Hayyan's spear darted forward to cover my flank every time I swung.

I turned to the right and sliced through another two nightbringers while Hayyan's spear flitted left, chopping off the tip of a hand that had creeped past my shield. Then I swung left, and Hayyan's spear darted right.

Nightbringers filled the room, but Valence's crystal couldn't have absorbed more life force. If we took out the nightbringers here, we could break the crystal.

I swung again, the magic dust floating through the air like hope.

But their black and red forms circled around Hayyan. We held them off from the front, but the sheer pressure of numbers drove them around us. Just as they had in Greenchapel.

"Hayyan—"a black limb hit mine, and I screamed. Hayyan chopped through it, but they had no warning of the nightbringer reaching for their back.

Bri's panga sliced through the nightbringer, his cape flying out behind him. Though slower than Hayyan, Bri fought with a focused intensity; his eyes caught every movement of the nightbringers and cut through each in quick succession.

I could feel the burns in my flesh, my bruised ribs from the golems, the sorrow of knowing Jon was dead. Yet I laughed. I couldn't understand it, but it filled the room.

Magic dust wafted through the air. It swirled in currents around my axe, each particle that dissipated replaced by a new one from the nightbringers I killed.

Then the ground shook. I flew backwards, sliding across the floor as I landed. My back hit the wall and knocked what little breath I had left out of me.

I looked up, and Hayyan leapt out of the range of the golem that attacked them. They tried to poke at its eyes, but the nightbringers reached for Hayyan's arms. All they could do was leap back, flicking their spear at the encroaching hands.

Bri retreated with them, keeping the nightbringers from circling behind. With every swing, he moved further from the crystal.

"That's it, run!" Valence cried, his voice still emerging from the golem. "Run knowing I will claim you in the end!"

I tried to stand, but my ribs throbbed, and I fell onto my hands and knees.

Carefully, I put one hoof on the ground, keeping my chest still, and then, finding a crack in the wall to use as leverage, I worked my way to my feet.

The nightbringers had pushed Hayyan and Bri beside me. I stood next to them and tried to drive us toward the crystal. I swung my axe, gritting my teeth through the pain in my side and chest. But the golem lumbered forward, flanked by the nightbringers. Combined, their speed and power were overwhelming.

"We've got to go down or we'll be crushed!" Hayyan shouted.

"This is our chance to be heroes—and if we fail, we die," Bri said.

The golem swung, forcing us to leap down the steps to keep out of its range.

"We've got no other options right now!" Hayyan said. "We can't stop it if we're dead!"

Bri grunted, but he had to jump back as the golem swung again. "All right, let's go!" he said.

The three of us turned and fled down the stairs, away from our one chance to survive.

RETREAT

E ven down the stairs, these nightbringers kept pace with us.
The floors flew by, a blur of purple objects.

"There!" Bri shouted. "Chase, Hayyan, help me with this!" His panga pointed to a large stone relief propped against the wall. We sprinted over, grabbed it, and dragged it to the stairs. We placed it against them just as the horde of black, red, and grey pressed up against it.

The golem looked at the relief blindly, as though it were another part of the tower that it simply had to maneuver around. But there was no space to do so. It paced on the step above the relief.

The nightbringers could climb over the relief, but we managed those. Hayyan and I stood at its base, our axe and spear swinging through them as Bri's arrows slowed them.

And yet, as we swung, the purply-pink light pulsed brighter and brighter.

"We need a new plan!" I shouted.

"We can beat them," Bri shouted as he loosed another arrow into the mass at the top of the stairs.

"We might have only minutes!" The top of the tower had been filled with nightbringers. How long it would take to kill them all?

My ribs ached as I swung my axe, my breaths shallow.

"Do we have any other options?" asked Hayyan. Their spear chopped through another hand.

I kept my shield up and scoured the room for something that could save us. Paintings, toys, harps, abacuses, slates, all bathed in the purple light of . . . the pillar. "We bring that pillar down, and we cut whatever is feeding that crystal. Maybe the whole tower!"

Bri glanced at the pillar as he drew and nocked an arrow. "Get to it, hero!" he said with a wheezing chuckle. "Hayyan, keep them off him."

"Got it!" Hayyan said. They stepped into the path of the nightbringers as I hurried to the pillar.

I pulled handful after handful of the blasting clay from its pouch. It squished between my fingers as I smeared it over the pillar. Done, I stepped back, picked up my axe, and pressed my hand against the clay.

"Blasting!" I shouted. Then, quieter: "Effusee."

The room shook. A metallic whine filled my ears. Though the magic only blasted inward, I staggered back, stunned. Dust filled the room. I choked and waved it away from the pillar. Had it worked?

Finally, the dust cleared, and I studied the pillar. The clay had blasted through a foot of stone. But the pillar still stood, another foot of uneven, chipped stone holding it upright.

The pulsing light from the floors beneath reached the wound and spewed purply-pink dust into the air; it dissolved into nothing. But above the wound, the pillar still gathered light and pumped it through the ceiling, up to the crystal above us. The pulses came slower than before—but shone just as bright. And were getting brighter.

Hayyan and Bri had been staggered by the explosion, but the stone relief was still in place, slowing the nightbringers. Hayyan recovered first, leaping away from their reaching arms. But a few struck Hayyan before they could get away.

Hayyan's spear slashed out, slicing through the nightbringers as they attacked them. But Hayyan favoured their right arm now. Splotches of charred skin covered their left arm.

Then the golem looked at me, and its gemstone eyes sparkled. Valence was looking through it.

"I shouldn't have left you to my creations, I see," he said, his voice hollow. "But this will not stop me. A few more minutes to gather my power, and then you will join me like the rest."

The golem lifted its arms into the air and slammed them through the stone relief, shattering it.

Nightbringers and the golem charged.

"Hayyan!" Bri shouted. "You go for the golem's eyes. I'll keep you clear!" He dropped his bow and dashed forward, his panga lifted high. He sliced through the nightbringers that flanked Hayyan as they poked at the golem's eyes.

The golem covered its face with one hand, and the spear struck the stone harmlessly. Blind, it swung wildly with its other hand. Hayyan and Bri dodged easily.

Valence clearly valued defence. That saved us from being overrun. But it also meant the golem wouldn't go down easy.

"Chase," Bri said, "we're counting on you!"

I looked back at the pillar. It was still so thick, and I had used all my blasting clay. But Bri and Hayyan were counting on me.

I dropped my shield and clasped my keratinous fingers against the stone. I took a deep breath and pushed with all my might.

My hooves screeched along the ground as the pillar remained in place. Still, I pushed until my breath was ragged and my ribs burned. Finally, I collapsed against the stone, spent.

Bri sliced through a nightbringer on Hayyan's right side. But as Hayyan poked at the golem's eyes, another nightbringer struck them on their left, burning away what little cloth remained. Hayyan squealed but kept fighting the golem as Bri hacked through that nightbringer, too.

I would not let them down.

I picked up my axe in both hands. I swung it against the stone.

The clang echoed through the room, though only a chip of stone broke off.

Again and again, I swung, though my arms burned and my ribs ached. I swung until my axeblade looked like a dented saw and the vibrations of each strike numbed my body part by part—fingers, arms, chest, head. I swung until my axe dropped from my stiff fingers.

I could hear Hayyan's delicate feet landing heavier and heavier, and Bri panting as he swung.

"However you damaged the pillar's surface, you're not going to break through its enchantments," Valence's hollow voice rang out. "You will die here."

I moved back as far as I could, lowered my head, and charged. The ground sped beneath me as I timed my leap. Five steps, three steps, one!

I flew, weightless. Then my left shoulder hit the stone. Steel squealed and stone crunched, and I collapsed to the ground in a heap. Pain shot through my shoulder and into my hand.

I tried to squeeze my hand, but more pain shot through my arm, and blood pooled beneath me. The stone had broken right through my armour. The jagged edge of metal cut into the soft flesh of my shoulder.

"Krek," I whispered. I took a breath and used my right hand to force myself to my knees.

"Chase!" I heard Hayyan shout, their back to me. "What's going on?" Then another squeal of pain and the smell of burnt flesh.

I tried to get to my feet, but my left arm wouldn't move, and I collapsed again. "Don't worry about me!" I shouted. I breathed and forced myself to rise to my feet.

I checked the pillar. The stone had chipped where I had hit it, but the damage was superficial. I would have to hit it a thousand times to break through.

I was going to die.

There was no escaping it now. But for some reason the thought did not fill me with dread.

All my life, I had sought *the rewards from obedience*. But today, I had chosen to take my light into the darkness, and I would die a thousand times to do so. Today, I would fight until my axe no longer swung, and then I would kick at them until my dying breath was suffused with spit and blood. Today, I would give everything I had to let Bri and Hayyan escape.

I looked through the window, at the same sun my mother had looked at so long ago. Of course my desires were wrapped in other people. Other people gave my life meaning. It was both selfless and selfish.

It was love.

I picked up my axe, leaving my shield on the ground. I forced myself to stand and gazed into the setting sun. I let its rays embrace me one last time, felt its heat along my face, and words came to my lips.

"I open myself to your light,
    And you fill me.

I open my body to your warm caress,
  And you melt idle lethargy with joy and love.
I open my mind to your radiant serenity,
  And you bore through petty distractions with devotion.
I open my soul to your inferno,
  And you incinerate the stupor of self-doubt with passion.

"With the ecstasy of joy and love,
  I will nurture my fire.
With the clarity of devotion,
  I will carry my flame into the darkness.
With the resolve of passion,
  I will burn and bring light to the world."

I had listened to them before. But this time, they filled me with a love so powerful my whole body burned with it. A love for Hayyan and Bri, for this beautiful world, for Delsaran, and even for Jon. I lived more in that moment than I could have in a thousand lifetimes.

I had only a few minutes, I knew. The pillar pulsed faster, and Bri and Hayyan were spent.

I smiled. They could kill me, torture me, make me say whatever they wanted, but I would be fire in the darkness.

I lifted my axe and readied myself to die.

"Hayyan, Bri!" I shouted. "Go! I will cover your escape!"

"That's suicide!" Bri shouted back.

"I will die on my terms and no one else's!"

Hayyan glanced at me, and then their mouth dropped.

"Chase," they said. "Your axe."

I looked up, and there it was.

The light.

My axe shone so bright that it drowned out everything. I couldn't even see the pulsing of the pillar behind it. It was radiant.

I laughed. It echoed back to me, deep and hearty.

"Ready to run?" I asked.

I swung.

My axe blasted through the pillar as though it were scarcely there, leaving a giant hole in its wake. Stone scraped against stone and rock cracked against rock. Rubble covered the floor and broke through the wall. Red sunlight streamed into the room.

I laughed again as the top of the pillar sank down. The ceiling warped as its support fell, the walls buckling around it.

The golem screamed and lurched to the side. Two quick thrusts, and Hayyan shattered its eyes.

The nightbringers continued to swarm forward, but Hayyan and Bri held their ground as I ran toward them.

Bri opened his mouth, but I could hear nothing but the rumble of stone.

We ran down the stairs as fast as we could, limping and exhausted. The building shook, and our feet bounced along the stones. Only the crashing rock behind us kept our pace up. Pieces of stone smashed through the floor, followed by nightbringers turning to dust as the large rocks broke them apart.

Something boomed through the walls, and we fell atop each other, tumbling down the stairs. I screamed as my wounded shoulder and bruised ribs hit each step.

Finally, I stopped, my back flat against the ground. I couldn't breathe; my ribs throbbed with every attempt. Hayyan lay atop me. I tried to wriggle out with my good arm but didn't have the strength.

Finally, Hayyan rolled off me. Slowly, shallowly, I could breathe.

The dust began to clear, and I watched the stairwell to see if anything followed us. If anything did, I had no strength to fight it. But we had saved Castulo. That would be enough.

The rumbling stopped and the ground became stable. I lay for I don't know how long, just watching the stairs. My breath calmed, and the pain of my wounds subsided.

We had survived.

I laughed again. Weak as the sound was, my whole body shook with it. I felt my laugh from my legs to my head.

We worked our way to our feet and opened the door. Rubble covered the market, and dust filled the air.

The top floors of the tower had fallen and shattered on impact. They had crushed the remainder of the golems beneath them. The rest of the tower had collapsed, and only the first two floors remained semi-intact. The surviving members of the guard peeked out behind the buildings at the edge of the marketplace.

Bri, Hayyan, and I helped each other climb over the rubble and looked over the city. The dust bleached the world of colour; buildings loomed greyly in the distance. And yet I felt more connected to them than I ever had before.

I had brought myself here, to this place, with these people. Everything I did shaped the world, just as the world shaped me. I took in its energy and made it my own, then I gave it back. I spread into the world until I could feel no difference between us.

And we were beautiful.

EPILOGUE

Hayyan's hand rested on the twisted head of my axe. Most of the metal had been sheared away by the pillar, but enough remained to serve as a marker for Delsaran. "I didn't know you for very long," they said, "but I thank you for always being someone I can be proud of."

I enveloped Hayyan's slender body in my own. My left shoulder protested, still tender after healers and rest, but that would never stop me. A moment later, Bri joined the hug, his arms going around Hayyan and resting on my back.

After a while, Hayyan relaxed their arms, and Bri and I broke the hug. Hayyan smiled, their eyes glistening.

"Thank you," they whispered.

"Chase?" Bri said.

I looked at the axe and the stone quill marker beside it. We had never found Jon's body, so both the graves were empty. But I felt them here, and that was what mattered.

I had buried Delsaran before. But now I knew what I needed to say to him—and Jon. I kneeled in front of their markers.

"Delsaran," I said to the axe, "you gave me a home when I needed one most. You taught me what makes life worth living. And you gave me the strength to defend my family.

"I will always love you."

"Jon," I said to the quill, "I spent my time with you yearning for something you could never provide. And you paid the people who stripped me from my family.

"Yet I can forgive you. When confronted with your part in evil, you sacrificed everything to set it right.

"In the end, you were better than you knew."

I continued kneeling, my eyes closed.

"I still don't have all the answers. I never will. We struggle to find our answers and hope they help others grow stronger." I reached out and held the axe in one hand and the quill in the other.

"I have grown stronger because of both of you."

I felt my chest rise and fall with my breath, then stood. I turned to Bri and Hayyan and held them tight against me. They both wrapped their arms around me while I cried.

They were tears of gratitude and regret, of grief and joy. And of belonging.

We stood there together, silently offering each other the comfort of our presence.

I had learned and done so much with them, yet, as my emotions cooled, I knew there was one more adventure for my family.

I stepped back, keeping a hand on each of their shoulders, and peering into their eyes. "I have another favour to ask of you."

Hayyan tilted their head quizzically, and Bri gave a half-smile, as though he knew what was coming.

"I want to find my mother."

"Sounds like an adventure," Hayyan said, their knuckles brushing back their hair.

"What hero wouldn't find his sidekick's mother?" Bri asked, crossing his arms with a smile.

I laughed.

I couldn't ask for a better family.

A week later, we set out.

We walked through the streets as they awakened in the light of dawn. Shutters opened and smoke puffed up from kitchen chimneys.

We didn't know exactly where we needed to go. We had searched the archives, but they didn't keep records of individual transactions. That was all right. She would stand out as much as I did. And this world was not as big as it seemed.

"After all," I said, and left the thought incomplete. Instead, I gazed into the rising sun as it turned from red to gold. Then I closed my eyes, and let its radiance fill me. Every part of me glowed in its light, and I felt at peace, yet full of desire. I rippled out into the world, my every action shaping it for eternity, and my thought completed itself.

"It's the same sun."

AUTHOR'S NOTE

Please consider leaving a review of this book. I'd love to hear your feedback, and I always strive to grow as a writer. Even a little comment, like, "I enjoyed reading this book a lot," helps me keep writing when the words don't want to come.

After all, writing is hard to do around a full-time job. For three years, I woke up before dawn to plot scenes, scribbled ideas in a notebook on the bus, and told family and friends that I really love them, but I can't see them right now because if I don't finish this chapter, I'll never get the book done.

Thank you to everyone who understood and celebrated my writing process. Who listened to me prattle on about Chase, Delsaran, Jon, Avinna, Andarta, Marcus, Hayyan, and Bri. Who read my various drafts and helped me see where the story needed to improve—or simply pushed me to keep writing. Korey, Spotty, BC8tive, Reid, Tristan, Beth, Charles, and Bowie, you all helped make this book happen.

Thank you to my partners, Fan, Dagda, and Kale, who always support me, and my parents, who put up with my awful first stories and bailed me out when my life-choices went awry.

Thank you to all those involved in the FWG, who gave me the writing community I needed. Special thanks to Khaki, who not only tirelessly promoted my art, but also gave me the support I needed when a piece of paper put me in crisis; without you I doubt I would ever have finished this.

Finally, thank you to Stephen Gordon, who taught me that economics is a way of seeing the world and our place in it.

My next novel, On the Shoulders of Demons, is already underway. On the Shoulders of Demons is historical fiction set in WWII Finland, so it's a bit of a change of pace. I've already travelled through Finland, researching the novel, and am excited to finish it. I hope you love it as much as I do.

I plan to return to Orachim and Chase someday and continue his adventure to find his mother.

Manufactured by Amazon.ca
Bolton, ON